RUSTLER'S HEART

The Kinnison Legacy, Book Two

BY

AMANDA MCINTYRE

&

Decadent Publishing Company
www.decadentpublishing.com

This book is a work of fiction. Names, characters, places, and incidents are the products of the author's imagination or used fictitiously. Any resemblance to actual events, locales or persons, living or dead, is entirely coincidental.

Rustler's Heart
Copyright 2014 by Amanda McIntyre
ISBN: 978-1-61333-637-3
Cover design by Sahara Kelly at P&N Graphics

Published by Decadent Publishing Company
www.decadentpublishing.com

Printed in the United States of America

~*Dedication*~

To all the virtuous, wise, and phenomenal women in my life,
you know who you are.

What readers are saying about
Rugged Hearts
The Kinnison Legacy Series – Book One

"A classic in the making."
~Kimberly, Book Obsessed Chicks Book Club

"Sexy, full-blown hotness, evenly written characters with the perfect amount of emotion that makes your heart swell with love and want."
~Vampires, Werewolves and Fairies, Oh My! Reviews On Rugged Hearts.

"To put it simply I love this book. These characters speak to your heart. I love their humor and their sexual chemistry."
~Rosemary, Amazon Reviews

"Ms. McIntyre always produces excellently written books with intriguing characters and heartwarming stories. I highly recommend this book and look forward to more stories in the Kinnison Legacy series."
~Margie, Amazon Book Reviews

"A sweet love story and a great comfort read!"
~Cocktails and Books

"A beautiful tale of love, loss, forgiveness of self, and hope for the future. Amanda McIntyre creates characters with a depth of emotion that grab you by the heart and keep you on the edge of your seat...A must read!"
~C.H. Admirand, Author of *A Wedding in Apple Grove.*

Chapter One

Rein wiped the sawdust on his jeans, grabbed his coffee mug and took a long swallow. He'd been up since before dawn, starting in on the details left to make the cabin ready by Friday. Since Aimee's arrival at the ranch on a semi-permanent basis, he'd spent more time on the cabins for more reasons than simply giving Wyatt and his soon-to-be bride privacy.

Wyatt had had a sudden change in heart about the project. He'd relinquished hold on his share of the ranch in order to collectively refinance and put more money into permits and materials to build the cabins and ready them for use. They'd given themselves a target date of two years to complete the project. Dalton, Michael Greyfeather, and Tyler Janzen from Janzen Plumbing and Heating, had come on board to help. That gave Rein the freedom to do what he loved, which was to design and build the rustic furniture that would grace the interior of each cabin.

However, Wyatt's unexpected news recently of a woman named Liberty who claimed to be their half-sister, had punched up the clock for completion of the sample cabin when she stated she needed a place to stay. The idea of having a half-sister hadn't settled well with Dalton, and frankly, Rein questioned why she would suddenly make contact after all of this time. Then again, she was only twenty-one, a kid in most respects, still fishing around to find her place in this world.

He stood for a moment at the screen door to the backyard and assessed whether there would be time to put in the brick patio he'd planned. The crisp spring air invigorated him. He loved to wake early and watch the sun climb high in the sky as it burned off the heavy mist over the mountains. Last night he had laid awake on the cot he'd brought down to the cabin and with the windows open, listened to the sounds of the creek and the forest that had become a part of him. He'd come to the ranch a grieving young man, bitter about the way things had turned out for him. But had found serenity and purpose in the ability to use his hands to create something from nature's bountiful resources. His Uncle Jed had taught him to give back to the land and to others. For him, it was the force that drove his inspiration to see his uncle's dream become a reality.

"I see you couldn't sleep, either." Dalton let the screen door slam behind him. He waved at the cot set up in the corner of the living room and made a beeline for the coffeemaker on the kitchen counter. "Looks like all the comforts of home. You may have a roommate soon if those two can't keep it down."

Rein had just finished shaving down the edges of the front door, preparing to place it in the frame when he had more help. "You're just in time. Grab those hinges, and help me get this in place."

He lifted the solid pine door from the sawhorses set up in the middle of the vacant cabin. With the three of them hard at work yesterday, they'd managed to get the bedrooms, bath and kitchen ready. Now, they only needed Tyler to come in and do his thing with the plumbing. Aimee, who'd gone to Billings for a final fit of her wedding dress, had offered to pick up a few necessities to complete a temporary living arrangement.

Rein slipped the shims into place and had Dalton hold the door steady while he drilled in the hinges. "You do look a bit haggard this morning, Dal." Rein smiled.

Dalton narrowed his bloodshot eyes on him. "We're going to need to get another cabin ready. Those two are like rabbits...fuckin' loud rabbits." He blew out a weary sigh.

Rein chuckled. Of course, he'd had a good night's sleep after he chose to come down to the cabin. He couldn't have been happier to see Wyatt rescued from the self-imposed prison he had been in. Aimee had changed him and for the better, but at the same time it sent a ripple of change through all their lives. Dalton as a rule, was less receptive to change. He liked continuity, liked for things to be certain way—in particular, his way. Though Rein knew that Dalton wished nothing but happiness for his brother.

"I was so damn tired this morning from listening to those two last night, I nearly forgot the new rule of not walking naked through the house." He scrunched his face and rubbed a hand over his unshaven cheek. "Aimee just about caught me in my birthday suit if it hadn't been for those throw things on the couch."

Rein shook his head and laughed. "Okay, let's see if this works." Dalton stepped back and Rein opened and shut the door several times to check for fit. He'd get around to adding a lock later. They'd never had any trouble with prowlers of the two-legged variety at the ranch—raccoons, snakes, and the occasional curious skunk were the worst offenders.

Dalton trudged across the room to refill his cup. "That about does it. Tyler said he'd be out later today." Rein flipped a switch and set to motion on an overhead light and fan combination in the middle of the living room ceiling. He studied it, pleased that it worked correctly. He shut the light off and looked at Dalton. "I think we're ready to haul the furniture up from the workshop."

Dalton eyed him. "You really like this, don't you?" he asked.

Rein picked up the broom, swept up the mess of sawdust he'd created, and dumped it into a box of debris ready to burn. "Getting to watch you work your ass off? Nothing makes me happier." He tossed Dalton a grin and received the finger in return.

"I mean this whole thing—this project." Dalton waved his hand over the room.

Rein shrugged. After he graduated with his business/marketing degree, he returned to the ranch to help by using his expertise. But when he discovered his uncle's private journal, outlining in specific detail his plans for the ranch, Rein found his purpose. He began to be inspired as he read his uncle's words and realized where Jed's ideas had taken root.

A civic-minded man, and a one of the community's leading businessmen, Jed taken on the task of raising three teen-age boys with no idea of where they were headed. He'd shown them through hard work what they were capable of. For Rein, that was designing and building with his hands. And he was damn good at what he did.

Rein leaned against the counter and gestured to Dalton with his cup. To his way of thinking there's no better smell in the world than fresh coffee and wood shavings. "I just love to build shit. You know that." He brushed off his comment and blew across his coffee.

"Yeah, but it's more than that, isn't it?" Dalton prodded.

Rein sighed and shrugged his shoulder. "I don't know, maybe. I'm twenty-nine. I have no kids, no wife...not even a prospect of one. I've spent most of my life on this ranch. Maybe this is what I can create to leave as my legacy. Besides, from a business standpoint, if we can get this off the ground and rent out these cabins, we could put the ranch on the map, as well as improve things for End of the Line. More tourists equals more money, equals more business, equals...."

"Yeah, I got it." Dalton sipped his coffee and studied him. "And you think that's what Jed wanted?"

Rein shrugged. "His journal talks a lot about it, yeah. He was part of the chamber as you remember. He always looked for new ideas to help, improve the community. You know that as well as me."

Dalton nodded. A short silence stretched between them. Rein narrowed his gaze and studied the man he considered a blood brother. "You aren't normally this chatty so early in the morning. What's up? I have a feeling you're leading up to whatever is really bugging you. So, let's have it. I haven't got all day to wrestle it out of you." He knew Dalton's moods like the back of his hand. Of the two brothers, he'd spent more time with Dalton, especially on business trips.

Rein had the book knowledge for running the ranch, while Dalton with his good old boy charm had a flair for schmoosing the socks off the stingiest buyer. If he had a downfall, it came in form of a bottle. More than once, Rein and Wyatt had to rescue Dalton from a late night bar episode, and he also realized that his troubled brother was still running from the demons in his past. Rein couldn't imagine what being abandoned by his mom would do to a kid, but he'd observed the results of in both men he considered older brothers.

Wyatt had spent years living as a recluse, earning the name of the town Grinch until last Christmas when persistent Aimee Worth and her second grade class got stranded at the ranch over the holiday. Like the beloved Christmas tale, people said Wyatt's heart grew three times its size during those sequestered days.

By the new year he and Aimee had announced their engagement. Their wedding became the talk of the town. He'd never seen Wyatt so happy. But the announcement seemed to do something to Dalton. He'd gotten more quiet and combined with his drinking Rein kept a closer eye on him. Watching Dalton made Rein realize how lucky he was. Unlike Wyatt and Dalton, abandoned by their mother, not even knowing who fathered them—at least Rein knew that his parents had loved him when they were alive. They'd cared about him, just as Jed had. Maybe that's why he felt such a vested interest in seeing this project through. Rein took a wild stab at what he thought might be Dalton's problem. "This is about Liberty, right?"

Dalton shrugged. "I don't know. It just doesn't feel right. I mean, what if this broad has some crazy vendetta, you know? I have no idea what kind of picture Eloise painted of me and Wyatt."

"Broad? You do realize you're talking about your half-sister, right? What are you saying...like she's going after you with a chainsaw in the middle of the night or something?" Rein laughed.

Dalton raised a brow.

"You've watched too many of those damn crime shows." He put his cup down and stretched out the kink in his back from sleeping on the cot. "I guess we'll find out a few days."

Dalton didn't respond.

"From what Wyatt told us,, it doesn't appear she's the serial killer type."

"That's just it. All he knows is what she told him. How do we know if any of it is true? How can we be certain of anyone's background that chooses to come here? That's my chief concern."

He considered Dalton's comments. "You make a valid point, and like Wyatt said, that is something we're going to have to address when we begin drawing up the rental agreements. But really, there is a multitude of ways to do a background check on someone if a person wanted to."

Dalton shrugged. "Yeah, you're right. I should do one on this Liberty chick. Good idea, bro." He reached over and slapped Rein on the shoulder.

He hated to feed into Dalton's obvious displeasure with Wyatt's decision to allow Liberty to come in and live off them until who knows when. But if little Miss Liberty thought for one minute she could stay here, eat their food, and use their services for free, she was in for a serious wakeup call.

Curious now, Rein rinsed out his cup and pulled on his work gloves. "Let me know what you find out. Meantime, let's head over and pick up that furniture before that storm blows in."

Dalton finished his cup and frowned as he followed him out the door. "In case you hadn't noticed, the sun is brilliant, and there isn't a cloud in the sky."

Rein fished the keys to his truck out of his pocket and eyed the sky. "Yeah, but I heard an owl outside the cabin last night."

Dalton rolled his eyes to the heavens. "Jeez, you and Wyatt and that damn American Indian mumbo-jumbo."

Rein just tossed him a smile.

CS

She checked her watch. Ticket in hand, Liberty waited on the scarred wood bench at the seedy bus station in the worst possible area of town. The clerk, safe behind her bulletproof glass and steel barred office, gazed out with a sullen face at the handful of passengers who waited for the nine-thirty bus. She looked again at the schedule. With a couple of transfers in Utah and Montana, she should arrive in Billings by midnight Friday. She'd packed in haste and brought only what she could carry in her oversized duffle. The rest she carried in a book bag and a small purse that she wore across the front of her body. The remainder of her last two paychecks she stashed in her boot.

She glanced at the couple beside her, newlyweds, she guessed from the lip-lock and their Vegas standard issue matching gold bands. Her gaze darted to the man across the aisle. He sat quietly watching the couple, as he clutched his briefcase close to his side. His expression was dour, as though he disapproved of their public affection. He caught Liberty's curious look and pulled his attaché closer to his side. Her choices for seating being severely limited, she shifted in her seat to look at the black retro wall clock and double-check the time. The soft whispers between the lovers reminded her of the mistake she'd almost made less than a year ago, just after her mother died.

CB

"I suppose you'll be expecting to move back home now that your mother's gone." She'd ridden in the funeral home's limousine, not by choice, but by request from her father. Funerals were as much a public appearance for her father, as any other he showed up for in Vegas. Nothing was left to chance. Appearances meant everything to him, they always had. Today he extended his benevolent hand to her...in his own, controlling way. Just as she'd seen him manipulate her mother the last years of her life. Liberty knew his game. She'd observed it all her life and only as she'd gotten older, had she come to resent and rebel against it.

"Did your housemaid quit again?" she tossed at him, watching row after row of headstones pass by as they left the burial plot. The dank, gray day mirrored her mood.

"Now, see there. That's what I'm talking about. I try to extend the olive branch, Liberty Belle, and you slap it out of my hand. The problem with you is that you never learned to appreciate everything I gave you."

She responded with a snorting laugh. "You mean, I didn't bow down and kiss your ass every time you decided to remember you had a family?"

His hand shot up, stopping short of smacking her across the face. She held his hard gaze with one of her own and saw the hate glittering in his black, soulless eyes. She'd discovered only recently the guilt her mother had carried inside her. Yet, for reasons unknown to Liberty, she wouldn't leave him. Liberty had heard her mother's pathetic attempts to appease his accusations from behind closed doors. She cringed at the anger in his voice, hated that her mother continued to take his abuse. So, she ran, as far away as possible. She'd never spoken to anyone about what she knew, fearing for her mother's safety. That was weeks ago. Her mother had found a way out and Liberty no longer needed to be afraid. "You touch me and I swear you'll be on the headlines of every paper in town." She kept her voice calm.

He eyed her a moment, chuckled, and then lowered his hand, straightening his Armani tie. "Just like your mother."

"Fortunately, she taught me more than you think, because I don't need you, and I don't need your money."

He looked straight ahead, indifferent, in control. "You'll feel differently when you see how much tuition is to that school of yours. Unfortunately, your mother, God-rest-her-soul, nullified her largely inadequate life insurance policy by virtue of how she chose to depart this world."

She leaned forward and tapped on the smoke-glass window shielding them from the driver. The window rolled down. "Pull over here and stop."

He looked over his shoulder, his expression hidden behind his mirrored sunglasses, but she caught the quirk at the corner of his mouth. She shook her head. There was nothing now holding her here. She wouldn't bow to her father's abusive control. "I said pull the goddamn car over."

"Don't be a fool. He can't just stop. There are well over a hundred cars following us."

Ignoring him, Liberty wrenched open the door. The limo came to an immediate stop. She stepped out, the mud from the rain earlier squishing into her heels and glanced back at the long procession of cars—not for her mother, but filled with those who bottom fed from her father's many Vegas enterprises. She bent down, holding to the door with one hand. "You know, you may have given me your seed, but you have never been a father."

He scooted across the seat; his dark, hateful gaze penetrated her heart. "You get back in the car, this instant you ungrateful—"

Liberty didn't wait for the rest. She slammed the door in his face. A small victory in the memory of her mother against the man who'd pushed her into an early grave. The window rolled down part way as the car lurched forward. "You'll regret this, Liberty. You could have had anything you wanted."

"At what price?" she called out as the car carried him away. She didn't care if anyone heard. They knew him well enough. She watched the faces of those in the cars that passed her. With each fearful glance, each look of pity, her resolve grew. Most of them lived in fear of his power. She'd just liberated herself from it. Overhead a clap of thunder reverberated in her chest and another rain shower washed down. She turned her face to the heavens, letting the water free her with its cleansing freshness. Pain, fear, and an unfathomable sense of loss, pierced her to the core. Her tears were lost in the torrent. But she opened her arms wide and spoke to the sky. "We're free, momma. We're finally free."

A few weeks later, she'd enrolled at the university, taking full responsibility for her loans. It hadn't taken her long to realize that the part-time waitress position wasn't going to be enough to make ends meet. Then, like an answer to her silent prayers, she met the devil in the form of exotic Angelo Patreous. He and his friends often stopped in late at night after some of the clubs on the strip had closed. In comparison to the bleary-eyed drunks that frequented the diner, he was a god—tall, exotic, and oozing charm. Well-to-do, he owned several clubs in the area, and much to Liberty's delight, he had no connection to her father. That alone appealed to her.

"You are a very lovely woman." He would tell her, showing off his white even smile. She accepted his flirtatious praise and his generous tips for the expert way she'd serve his pancakes. One thing led to another and she found herself invited to one of his clubs, where he introduced her to his dancers. A few weeks later, she found herself headlining and earning enough to pay off what loans she'd accumulated, rent a nice apartment and convince herself as long as she could dance she didn't need college.

❧

"Do you have change for a dollar?"

The fresh-faced, new bride pulled Liberty from her reverie. "Oh, sorry. No. Maybe the attendant can help you?"

"Sure, thanks." Her lover could barely let go of her as she struggled to stand.

Liberty readjusted her things, aware that the movement from the young woman had once more stirred the putrid air filtered in from unclean bathrooms. The arrogant looking dark-haired lady behind her shifted in her seat, assaulting Liberty with her sickly, sweet perfume. She spied a streetlight outside the murky, picture window, but decided she'd be safer inside, despite the intrusion to her senses.

Liberty watched as the giggling young woman return to her amorous husband. He wasted no time as he slipped into the men's bathroom, and returned with a handful of condoms.

She looked away. Their reckless behavior reminded her too much of how she and Angelo once were. She'd been with him nearly three years, accepting the fact that his cut of the dancers wages were to help pay for overhead, new props, and costuming. She discovered though, through the grapevine that he possessed an expensive cocaine habit, and while he never made it obvious, she began to see the signs—the paranoia, the sleeplessness, the abuse. Angelo wouldn't be happy when he found out that she'd snuck in his office and taken back her twenty percent cut. If she could get to this remote ranch, she'd have enough time to figure out what to do next.

She drew her jacket closer together and folded her arms over her chest as she looked around her. A low rumble echoed in the deserted streets, and she held her breath until the bus turned the corner. She released a sigh with the sound of its airbrakes as it pulled into the garage. The sooner she put some distance between her and this town, the better off she'd be.

"May I get this for you?" The dark-eyed man stood when she did. Liberty grabbed her duffle and swung it over her shoulder with the practiced ease of a combat soldier. Strength and agility were the rewards of her profession. "Thank you, no. I've got it." She walked head high to the bus, and tossed it into the luggage compartment without the driver's assistance.

"One bag, ma'am?" he queried and held out his hand for her ticket and ID She produced the information and waited as he eyed her and then the license. "That was taken six years ago."

"Don't forget to renew before your birthday." He smiled and handed it back to her. "Welcome aboard. Your first transfer will be in Salt Lake at our six-fifty a.m. stop."

She nodded her thanks, climbed onto the bus and searched for a quiet spot to sit where she wouldn't be disturbed. She moved toward the back, away from the passengers at the front of the bus, and dropped her bag in the seat next to her. The dark-eyed man glanced at her, but ended up taking the seat next to the woman with the heavy perfume. The amorous couple, on the other hand, giggled and pawed at each other as they passed by her to sit at the very back of the bus.

It could be an interesting next few hours.

She pulled out her iPod, put in her ear buds and scanned through her music until she found *Heart's Greatest Hits*.

Sometime later, startled awake by an odd sound, she realized one of her ear buds had slipped out. Her cheek felt cool to the touch, from where she'd slept with her face pressed against the window. Disoriented, she blinked, trying to determine how long she'd slept. She glanced at her watch, seeing the late hour and remembered that she was heading to god-knows-where-Montana. She peered down the aisle. Everyone on the bus, except the young couple in the back, were asleep.

"Aw honey, that's it," the male voice hissed quietly. A feminine sigh and a soft groan followed.

She didn't need to look back to know anymore. Liberty shook her head. Maybe she was jealous. At least they had each other and despite their lack of propriety, they were clearly in love. Even so, she hoped that they'd get off at the next stop. A quiet male groan caused her to chuckle.

Or maybe sooner.

She repositioned the ear bud to stifle the sounds of their lovemaking and checked her phone. There were two missed calls both from Elaina, a friend of hers from work. She quickly punched in a text.

Are you home, and is everything okay? Has Angelo said anything to you?

A few moments passed before she received a text in response. *He did. But since you refused to say where you were going, it didn't take long for him to give up. I don't trust him, Libby. If cellphones can be traced, he'll know who to pay to make it happen.*

Ca

By the time they pulled into Salt Lake, Liberty had deleted all contacts, messages, and calls received. Dropping her phone in an empty coffee cup, she replaced the plastic lid before discarding it in the trash outside the restaurant. She climbed on her transfer bus, glad that the couple, as well as the dark-eyed man who gave her the creeps, stayed on the other bus, bound for points further east.

She leaned her head against the window and watched the limitless blue sky give way to a dusty twilight. Dozing off and on, she awoke to a black velvet sky sprinkled liberally with stars. There were few times she could count that she'd seen the sky awash with stars. The garish lights of Vegas always blocked them from view. Her eyes drifted shut and the gentle rocking motion of the bus lulled her to sleep.

Chapter Two

"Nope. I made it clear, Wyatt. You invited her. She's your responsibility."

"I forgot that Aimee had scheduled dinner tonight with Pastor Tony and his wife. Come on, man. I just need you to go pick her up at the bus depot."

"Sorry, I have plans."

"Dammit, Dalton. You stubborn son of a...." Wyatt paced the living room, Sadie dutifully at his heels.

Rein peeped open an eye. He'd laid down in the living room, exhausted and unable to haul himself upright to shower after they had moved all the furniture into the cabin. But he'd listened to this tirade for the better part of fifteen minutes. Enough was enough. "You two sound like bitchy, old women," he mumbled.

"Shut up," they replied in tandem.

He turned to his side and snuggled with the throw pillow on the couch.

"Wait. I'm sorry, Rein. Have you got plans for tonight?"

"You're looking at them, Wyatt. I've busted my butt for the last forty-eight hours trying to get that cabin into shape for your sister."

"Half-sister," Dalton interjected.

"Dalton, do you intend to be an ass the entire time she's

here?" Wyatt asked. "I actually thought that of the two of you, you would be the more open-minded."

"Thanks, Wyatt," Rein mumbled into the pillow. Had he the energy, he might have smacked his ungrateful brother.

"Fine, I'll call Aimee and tell her we have to reschedule."

Rein waited a heartbeat for Dalton's apology. Meantime, he fought the urge to knock Dalton's head off. "Would it kill you to drive down to Billings?" He looked at Dalton through blurry eyes.

"I told you. I have plans." Dalton growled.

"Jesus. Criminy. Fine, I'll go." Rein pushed to his feet, winced and grabbed his lower back. Four-thirty in the afternoon, and he felt like an eighty-five year old man with arthritis.

"Where the hell is she supposed to be?"

Wyatt slapped his hand on Rein's shoulder. "You're a lifesaver, man. Thanks."

"Here's the number of the bus and there is her cellphone number. She gets in at eleven-fifteen. The bus station's not in the best part of town, so don't be late. I don't want her to sit alone down there."

Rein nodded, took the paper, and stuffed it into his pocket.

"You know, in case you're interested, I've been doing a little research on our mysterious half-sister," Dalton stated. He moved Jed's desk and flipped open the laptop.

"Give it a rest, Dalton," Wyatt said.

"Don't you want to hear what I found out?"

"No," Wyatt barked in response.

"Yes," Rein countered. "What did you find out?"

Dalton settled back in the chair and pointed at the screen. "Says here that she attended the University of Nevada, interior design program."

"I told you that." Wyatt folded his arms over his chest.

"Just verifying, bro." Dalton glanced over the screen at his brother. "Doesn't say whether she graduated."

"Anything else?" Rein asked

Dalton frowned, his dark brows pressed together as he studied the information. "It gives her last known address. It looks like an apartment." He paused then looked at Wyatt. "Parents, deceased—mother, Eloise."

Wyatt spread his arms. "There, are you happy?"

"Yeah, well there's something else here that you might find interesting."

Wyatt shook his head.

Rein moved slowly, favoring his back as he walked over and stood behind Dalton.

"It says her last place of employment was the Kit Kat Club."

"Did you search engine it?" Rein nudged him.

Dalton tossed him a smug grin and hit one of the keys. A slow vampy, bump and grind tune blasted from the site, which left little doubt to the type of entertainment the club offered. If that wasn't enough, the pictures of voluptuous women with triple-X covering the strategic parts of their bodies cinched any remaining doubt. Rein searched the faces and had a hard enough time trying to determine which of them might be Liberty. He looked up and met Wyatt's steely gaze. "None of them look young enough to be her." This unexpected news did little to ease the already mounting tension between Wyatt and Dalton.

"She said she quit school and had her reasons. We don't know what circumstances drove her to take a job there," Wyatt said calmly.

"And she very well might have been a cocktail waitress or bartender." Rein jumped on that positive bandwagon, hoping to diffuse the ticking bomb in the room. "Hell, they have tons of female bartenders in Vegas."

"Turn it off, Dalton. You're through with your investigation," Wyatt warned.

Rein looked from one man to the other. There were few times that Wyatt took that particular tone with anyone, much less Dalton. He clapped his hands once. "I'm going to go take a shower and grab something to eat. I need to stop by Tyler's and talk to him about the plumbing in one of the cabins. Then I'll head down to Billings." Rein looked at Dalton. "If you want to join me, you are certainly welcome."

Dalton dropped the lid to the laptop. "Nope." He pushed away from the desk. "Since one of us has dinner plans, I guess the other one is in charge of chores." Grabbing his cap and jacket, he stomped out the door. Rein glanced at Wyatt who stood staring where Dalton had been.

"I don't think until this moment, I realized how wrapped tight to the point of selfish I was about my mom and what she did to us." His gaze met Rein's. "I think maybe Dalton's going to have a tougher time letting go of all that he's been through." He sighed, clearly concerned over his brother's welfare. "I appreciate you doing this."

"He'll come around. Give him time. He's just protecting the only family he's got."

෬

Rein had to remind himself of that a few short hours later. He checked his watch again—eleven o'clock. He hadn't ridden a bus, much less heard of many who'd for opted that mode of travel, except maybe charter tours of senior citizens. With the numerous changes and faster means of transportation, the majority of bus stations fell into a state of disrepair, and the one he waited at had to be at the top of that list. As a rule, very little made him uncomfortable. More a lover, than a fighter, he could still hold his own. He scanned the dimly lit station. The flickering of can fires made by vagrants dotted the area outside the stations chain link fence. Though he doubted that would keep them from entering the depot. The place gave him the creeps, not to mention it made him damn curious as to the type of woman who'd choose this form of travel at this hour. She either was extremely naïve or had the balls of a prize bull, with a degree in some type of martial arts added as a plus.

The sound of the bus brought his head up from the game on his iPhone. He pulled out the number Wyatt gave him and dialed it not once, but twice, and received her voice mail. She sounded a whole lot older than twenty-one. He sat in his truck and watched each person climb off the bus with the idea that when she appeared, he'd instantly recognize her. Only five people departed. One man made a hasty exit to his parked car and another checked something on his phone before he stepped to the street to hail a cab. The rest entered the station, but in the low light, he couldn't see well. He tapped his fingers on the steering wheel, pocketed his phone and keys, and hopped from his truck, his eyes peeled as he approached the station.

Stepping inside, his senses were immediately challenged by the acrid smell of urine, bleach, and the sight of overstuffed trash bins. One person crouched in front of a vending machine awaiting his order, while another man studied a wall map. Unless Liberty wore a man's disguise, there were no other people in the station.

He pushed his hat up, stepped outside, grateful for the fresh air though it mingled with a heavy diesel smell. Maybe she hadn't gotten off the bus yet. "Excuse me." He walked over and stood at the base of the open bus door. The driver jotted something down on his clipboard. "Has everyone departed from the bus?"

The man did a quick glance down the aisle and nodded. "No one left onboard. You check the bathrooms inside?"

"Wyatt?"

That was definitely the voice from the voicemail. It skirted up his neck like silky fingers and made the tiny hairs stand on end. He turned to face her. "I must have just missed you—" The words halted with his brain. Cold dead. He blinked, afraid he might be too tired, and seeing things. "Are you...Liberty?" He tried not to sound incredulous.

"I am," she replied as though nothing at all appeared out of the ordinary. She had a massive green duffle bag hooked over one shoulder. His gaze traveled down her long black leather trench coat, to the triple-buckled motorcycle boots on her feet. Admittedly, he had a moment, though very brief, when he wondered what she wore under that coat, but he ran like a man with his hair on fire away from the thought. And tried to unglue his tongue from the roof of his mouth.

"My uh, name is Rein." He chuckled and tried to cover it with a cough as he eyed her hair. Though dark like Wyatt and Dalton's, it hung loose and straight to her shoulders. But it was the brilliant neon blue highlight that streaked down one side that he couldn't stop staring at. Her deep brown eyes—also a family trait—regarded him with equal curiosity. *A wig?* He shook his head, realizing he hadn't finished telling her his name. "Rein Mackenzie."

Her dark brows pinched together and for a split second, he saw the resemblance to Dalton. Something he would never reveal to him.

"Oh, you're the guy Wyatt talked about. Jed's nephew." She peered at him.

He figured that he had to look about as strange to her in his conventional cowboy wear, as she did to him. He reminded himself of that as he pointed to the truck and followed her. The folks back home were in for quite a treat and Halloween was months away.

"Here let me take that," he offered and reached for her duffle.

"Thanks." She relinquished it to him. He did a double take when he caught the flash of silver on her tongue.

"Uh, are you hungry?" He squinted, trying to see when she spoke, if her tongue was really pierced. "It's about an hour back to the ranch. Probably someplace near that's open all night." Preferably a drive-through, though he kept the thought to himself.

"That'd be great. I'm famished," she said as she struggled free of her coat. Rein dropped her bag in the back of the truck and waited to assist her into the cab. His gaze fell to her backside bent over the front seat and what was left of her black mini skirt and spandex leggings. She handled the look well, given it appeared she had legs a mile long. She stuffed her coat up into the cab and jerked down her black hoody sporting a faded *Guns & Roses* insignia emblazoned the back He caught a flash of skin above her waistband, just enough to make him feel guilty for wanting to see if she bore any tattoos. He'd bet money that she had one, if not more. First impression, she looked like the lead in an R-rated vampire slayer movie.

"Be careful. Watch your step." He gave himself a mental slap and hurried forward to help her in the cab. She gingerly grabbed the bar and hauled herself up gracefully into the seat.

"Did you happen to get my text messages?"

"Nope, I'm afraid not."

"Is there someone back home that needs to know you're here?"

"No, there isn't." She narrowed her gaze on him. "Mr. Mackenzie, in case you hadn't noticed, I'm not twelve years old."

As if he needed to be reminded of the interest she sparked in him. He brushed it off as her eccentricity. "Right." He shut the door, fished for his iPhone, and frantically texted Wyatt as he walked around to the driver's side. He wanted to make damn sure they were awake when they arrived back at the ranch. *Going to stop for a bite to eat, and then head home.* He paused at the door and rubbed his hand over his mouth, a nervous habit when he found himself perplexed by something. With a sigh, he climbed into the truck and busied himself with his seat belt.

"Who were you texting?" she queried.

"Wyatt. Just to let him know you were safe and sound."

"He was worried? That's so big brother of him." She grinned. "By the way, my name is Liberty...Liberty Belle."

Rein glanced at the young woman who looked tough enough to spit nails. "No last name, or is it Belle?" Her mascara-laden, coffee-colored eyes met his. She wore far too much in his opinion. But he had to give her credit, while the overall effect seemed a little dark...no...make that *a lot* dark, it was oddly sexy on her. Rein batted away the silly notion. *What? Sexy? Where'd that come from?*

"No, Belle is my middle name, and also my stage name. Both my parents were in the business. My full name is Liberty Belle Stenapolas."

He toyed with pursuing the topic of her vocation, but decided her brothers should be the ones to delve into that first. He kept his focus straight ahead and swatted away the myriad of questions that kept popping up in his brain.

"Hey, are you okay?" She leaned toward him and searched his face. "Are you sure you know how to get us out of here?"

Rein blinked, snapping out of his reverie. He started up his truck and shifted into gear. He knew easily how get them out of there with no trouble. But more to the point, what kind of trouble was he bringing home to Last Hope Ranch?

ය

She understood now what the monkeys in the zoo felt like. Liberty averted her eyes from the blatant stare of the ruggedly handsome, dark-haired man she guessed was her older stepbrother, Wyatt. At his side stood a petite blonde, presumably his fiancée. Rein, who'd offered to bring in her bag, placed it at her feet. He glanced at her and cleared his throat. "Is someone going to say something?" He shot a pointed look to the other man, startling him from his reverie.

"Forgive me." The blonde-haired woman stepped forward and offered her hand. "I'm Aimee, Wyatt's fiancée. Welcome to the ranch." She had a kind face with gentle blue eyes.

"Thank you." Liberty accepted her hand and turned her focus on the man who had yet to speak. "I'm guessing then that you must be, Wyatt?" It was an awkward moment to meet the closest thing to a brother that she had on this earth.

He gave a short nod, but made no overt attempt to welcome her. She caught him assessing her clothing. "Not really what you expected, right? I promise I don't drink blood or play with sharp objects." She smiled and extended her hand when he hadn't yet.

He shot a look toward his fiancée who responded with a bright smile. He accepted Liberty's hand and pulled her into a bear hug. Her body stiffened, unprepared for the blatant show of affection. "Okay, there cowboy," she muttered through his grip.

"Welcome to our home." He gave her a quick squeeze.

"Oh!" she squeaked in surprise at the gesture. "It's certainly nice of you to have me."

He stepped away as did she, in nervous embarrassment. Liberty took a deep breath and released it. Given his chilly tone on the phone, she'd not expected a warm reception from anyone, least of all Wyatt. Not used to being nervous, she realized her hands were clammy. Looking to make conversation, she asked, "Where's Dalton? Does he go by Dalton, or Dalt?" She shrugged.

Rein ignored Wyatt's displeased look. "Dalton's not here right now. You'll meet him tomorrow at breakfast."

Breakfast? After the night she'd had? "Maybe lunch." She chuckled. Both men turned their stoic expressions on her. "Or breakfast and I bet it's hearty." She noted Aimee turning her head to cover a smile. She cleared her throat and straightened.

"Well, it's pretty late. I'd be happy to show you to your—"

"She can stay in my room. I'm already halfway moved into the cabin." Rein stepped around her. "I just need to pick up a few things," he said.

"Well, that's right neighborly of you, Rein," Aimee stated as he strode past her. He stopped, turning his blue-eyed gaze on Aimee. He had an ornery smirk on his face.

"No trouble at all, ma'am" He tipped his head slightly and Liberty's stomach did a little flip. His gaze rolled to hers. "Are you a light sleeper?" he asked.

Aimee blushed, her eyes riveted to the floor.

Liberty caught the steely look of warning Wyatt cast at Rein. It didn't take a rocket scientist to figure out what he was talking about. It felt good to be included in the teasing. "I sleep like the dead," she said, holding back a smile.

The corner of Rein's mouth lifted as they connected with the harmless joke. "Good thing," he muttered and disappeared down the hallway.

After Rein had graciously taken her bags to his room, Liberty sat on the edge of the massive king-size bed, while Aimee moved about the room, straightening up as she explained how she and Wyatt met. She couldn't dismiss however, the fact that her step-brother had followed Rein out the door, claiming he'd help Rein with the horses. But she had a gut feeling they wanted to discuss her in private. Aimee, on the other hand, treated her like they were old friends.

"I'm so glad you're here before the wedding. I think it's important to have your family near on the special moments in your life." She stripped the bed and tossed Liberty a set of clean sheets. "This will go faster if I enlist your help. Do you mind?"

"Not at all." Liberty positioned herself on the other side of the bed, thinking how well it fit the rugged-looking man who slept in it. "So, what's Rein's story?" she asked casually. Though curious to find out what she knew about her brother's upbringing, Liberty decided that topic they'd eventually tackle. Her mother always spoke lovingly about her sons, how Jed would have raised them like the gentleman he was. But given Wyatt's hesitant welcome and Dalton's marked absence, she surmised that the memories about the mother they shared were not nearly as poignant.

Liberty snapped the sheet open, listening as Aimee told her about Rein.

"Rein was young when his parents were killed in car accident. And his uncle, Jed Kinnison, the man who married your mom, had adopted Wyatt and Dalton. As it happened, the three boys were very close in age when life threw them together." She paused, her gaze darting to Liberty. "I hope that doesn't sound too insensitive. But I'm sure you can imagine how devastated they were."

"And probably angry. For what it's worth, she never shared the details with me. But from what I know, I think there were many times she regretted her decision to leave here. My father can be...shall we say, very convincing when he wants something." Liberty continued as she tucked in the corner of the sheet. "She often said that she knew Mr. Kinnison would raise the boys right." She stood for a moment, seeing her mother's face when she talked about the ranch. "I don't think she felt she'd done well by them. She suffered from low self-esteem. My father fed on that." Liberty met Aimee's kind gaze. "I think she thought leaving the boys here was the best choice she had."

Aimee nodded as though she understood. "Wyatt told me that Jed built this ranch in hope of having a big family one day. Everyone who knew him felt him to be a generous man. Big-hearted, he gave to the community in large and small ways. When he adopted the boys, I believe he felt he'd found his family. He raised them as his own, taught them about the ranch, instilled in them a responsibility and pride about it. It wasn't until recently that Rein found his uncle's journal outlining his dream to make the place a working ranch for people needing a place to heal. Now, together, the three of them are setting out to make it a reality." Aimee tossed a fluffed pillow to her. Liberty caught the residual whiff of fresh linen and a musky male scent embedded in the fabric. For a brief moment, she held it against her chest, imagining Rein's sexy face against it as he slept. She watched as Aimee flitted about the room, tucking Rein's things in the closet. She stepped back, pleased with her progress.

"There. I'll just set out some fresh towels in the bathroom."

Liberty's gaze started to follow her to the private bathroom, but instead she caught her reflection in large mirror hanging over the handmade dresser. She stared at her image. Clearly, not the typical sister they might've expected. With her raven hair, blood red lipstick and tongue piercing, even Liberty thought she looked out of place. At least she'd given them something to talk about.

She hauled her duffle bag onto the bench at the end of the bed and scanned the room, noting the stark difference from the sleek chrome and glass world she'd come from. Everything around her had the quality of handmade craftsmanship—from the rough-hewn, polished bedposts made from the trunks of small trees, to the exquisite carved detail of the dresser and nightstands. Each section shone with a rich amber lacquer that brought out the beauty of the wood. The room, the house, the décor, it all smacked of old family comfort and wealth— plenty of it—done country-style. She'd seen her share of rhinestone cowboys that head-lined the shows on the strip. But stage persona was far different than the real deal. Liberty ran her hand down the smooth bedpost and thought of the heart that had gone into its creation.

"Beautiful, isn't it?" Aimee returned from the hallway. "Rein made every stick of furniture in this room and a lot of it throughout the house. He's an amazing carpenter."

"Wow," the word slipped from her mouth without thinking. She eyed the room with renewed interest. She pointed to an overstuffed reading chair and ottoman placed in front of a set of French doors leading outside. Beside it sat a low table with a brass, tiffany reading lamp, perfect for a cup of coffee and a good book on a rainy day. She walked over and smoothed her hand over the soft navy and ecru ticking. "Did he build this as well?"

"Yep." Aimee nodded as she walked over and pushed the window open a crack. "The fresh air out here will help you sleep like a baby."

Liberty came around to the end of the bed and perched on the edge of the blanket bench. "Tonight, or should I say this morning? Either way, I don't think that'll be a problem."

"Well, I guess I'll say good night, and we'll see you in a few hours." Aimee started to leave.

"Aimee," Liberty said, stopping her. "Thank you. I got the feeling that Rein and Wyatt aren't exactly overjoyed with my being here. It kind of makes me wonder," she chuckled, "why you're being so nice to me?" Averting from Aimee's curious gaze, she focused on the bench, running her fingers over the brass tacks holding the cushion in place. Every burnished upholstery tack appeared perfectly measured. The sign of a man who liked tradition—a no-nonsense kind of guy. Wyatt, she had yet to get to know. Rein had been like an open book from the moment he said her name. The intonation in his voice spoke volumes of what he thought of her, and it hadn't been very flattering.

Aimee leaned against the doorframe and smiled. She had a faraway look in her eye. "I had a twin sister."

Liberty looked up, narrowing her gaze on the woman.

"It's not easy to talk about, but it's important that I do. I really owe her more for my life and how it's turned out." She cleared her throat and straightened. "A few years ago, she was killed in a car accident. She and I had different plans. She wanted to teach, preferably in a rural community in need of good teachers. I wanted the city life, the corporate world, corner office, the whole deal. After her death, I re-evaluated my life, what was important to me and decided to get my teaching degree. I looked at the towns she'd researched—her top twenty list—" Aimee smiled. "And chose End of the Line." She shrugged. "Who knew?"

Liberty listened intently, finding the woman's courage and sacrifice amazing. No wonder Wyatt fell for her so fast. "I don't know if I could do that," Liberty said "But, what about your goals?"

Aimee's eyes were misty, making Liberty uncomfortable that she'd asked.

"They changed. I started seeing life differently. So I made my choices, and by some quirk of fate, to which I owe a great deal to my second-grade class of last year, I met Wyatt. Had we not ended up stranded—"

"Stranded?"

Aimee dismissed the topic with a wave of her hand. "It's late and that's another story I'll share with you sometime over a glass of wine. Right now, you need some rest." Her gaze met Liberty's. "You asked why I was being nice. One reason is that I'm just damn giddy to have another female in the house." She grinned as she batted away the tears escaping her eyes. "Sleep well."

CЗ

Liberty stared at her reflection in the bathroom mirror. Despite the hot shower she'd hoped would revive her, her eyes remained puffy, rimmed with dark shadows. As though catapulted into a Disney movie, the birds outside her window had begun their melodious racket long before the sun peeked through the curtains. That, and the tossing and turning from the scent on Rein's pillow and the strange quiet out in the country had made it difficult to fall asleep.

A short rap sounded on the outer bedroom door. She peered out of the bathroom. "Who is it?"

"Rein. Aimee sent me to tell you breakfast is about ready."

"Thank you. I'll be right out." She waited another moment, expecting a response and when none followed, she figured he'd gone. She grabbed a towel and wrapping it around her, stepped into the bedroom. A yelp escaped her throat and she froze in place. There stood Rein, struggling to unhook a shirt from the back of the door. He tilted his head, trying gallantly to avert his eyes.

"Damn. Sorry." He muttered at the door. "I thought I could sneak in here and get my shirt."

Liberty found the scene charming. "You might have said you needed something." She pushed the wet hair from her face, enjoying how he seemed genuinely nervous. Part of her wondered what he'd do if she dropped the towel.

"Sorry, I'll just—" *Thunk.* "God-blessed, son-of-a—" He stopped short his expletive and held his hand to his head. He slammed the door behind him and the corner of her mouth lifted. This was going to be an interesting visit. Opting for a running bra under her cami, she pulled on old sweatshirt that hung well below her plaid men's boxer shorts. She followed the heavenly smell of bacon frying to the dining room, where the table was set, but no one appeared to be around.

"Oh good morning," Aimee smiled as she carried a platter laden with bacon and link sausages to the table. It appeared enough to feed an army.

"Can I help?" Liberty eyed the plate, feeling her arteries tremble. Coffee, a banana, and maybe a yogurt smoothie was her usual fare for breakfast.

"Wyatt could probably use a hand. He's in there cooking up a storm. Hope you have an appetite this morning. There's a bunch of guys coming out today to help work on setting up for the wedding. My guess he's taking out his jitters by cooking too much."

Aimee's eyes sparkled as she talked about her special day. But Liberty noticed the dark circles beneath those eyes and wondered how much stress Aimee carried. "You think he needs me underfoot in there?"

She placed the tray on the table and took a deep breath as she lifted her gaze. Liberty noted an odd look flicker through her eyes. She blinked a couple of times, shook her head and took a deep breath, releasing it slow. "Are you okay?" she asked.

Aimee nodded. "Yeah, I need a bit of fresh air. If you could go help in there, I'm going to step out on the porch, just for a minute."

Liberty nodded and watched her leave. Her hesitancy to face Wyatt alone however, kept her feet frozen in place. "Liberty?" She turned to face Aimee, who had her arms wrapped around her middle. Her eyes shimmered in her pale face. "Wyatt's kind of quiet until he gets to know you. But he's a good man, Liberty. Loving, fair, and kind. Be patient. You'll see it's worth the effort of breaking through the hard exterior."

Her chief concern wasn't Wyatt. What had plagued her sleep had been Rein's look of disapproval when they first met, and the thought of Angelo's temper when he discovered she'd left. She had so much to overcome and welcomed Aimee's instantaneous friendship, but she wondered what it would take to be accepted by Rein, Wyatt, and Dalton. "If you say so." She started toward the kitchen.

"Hey Liberty?" Aimee called quietly.

"Yeah?" She glanced at the kind woman.

"You're very pretty, too. Without the make-up. I didn't notice last night how your eyes are the same color as Wyatt and Dalton's."

Liberty smiled and ducked her head as she entered the kitchen. Wyatt eyed her and returned to flipping pancakes.

"Sleep well?"

"It's really quiet out here. I'm not used to that," she replied.

His gaze took her in. "I suspect you'll have a lot of things to get used to while you're here."

The backdoor opened, and Rein stepped in. He tried to hide his startled expression, but those clear blue eyes were as open as a book. In a hurry it seemed, he passed them with but a nod and disappeared in to the other room. She could hear him chatting with Aimee, asking whether someone named Sally would be stopping by today to discuss the wedding.

Liberty folded her arms across her chest and dove in. "I didn't get the chance to really congratulate you properly about your engagement. I realize I've missed out on all the preparations, but I'd like to be of help. Maybe I could do something nice for the both of you."

The muscle of his clean-shaven jaw ticked as he flipped another pancake. "That's much appreciated, but you being here is quite enough." He handed her a platter of pancakes.

"Can you take these to the dining room? The guys ought to be here soon."

Mulling over his remark, she carried the plate in and found Rein seated at the table, perusing the morning paper. His gaze met hers, locking for a moment before he put the paper down and motioned her closer. Thinking it pancakes he wanted, she held out the plate, surprised when his hand closed around her wrist. He took the plate from her hand and set it aside, and holding her gaze, leaned forward until their noses nearly touched. Liberty's heart thudded in her chest. Those piercing eyes, the color of a brilliant summer day, held hers.

"Just a little advice." He spoke low, the sound of it sending a shiver across her shoulders. She pressed her lips together, trying not to imagine what his lips might taste like. He smiled and though pleasant, her gut cautioned against becoming too comfortable around him.

"Around here, we dress before breakfast." Leaving wide open the implication that he knew fully she'd been a stripper in Vegas. Just the same, she wasn't going to let this cowboy or anyone else make her feel small. She reached out to trace the front collar of his snap shirt with her black polished fingernail. "Thanks for the tip."

"You're welcome," he replied, his body stiffening as she moved closer, her cheek brushing his.

"This is more clothes than I usually wear before breakfast," she whispered in his ear, straightening. Her lip curled when his gaze darted to hers with a flicker of a challenge. "You couldn't handle it, cowboy." She answered that surprised expression and watched with pleasure as his mouth gaped, but he had no response. There might be eight years difference between them, but damn if they weren't going to get a few things straight between them—namely, she didn't take well to being bossed around and she wasn't his baby sister.

Chapter Three

A few moments later, when she returned in jeans and a black t-shirt with the rhinestone studding, "Vegas," emblazoned across her chest, she found several men seated at the table. There were two spots left—one next to Wyatt, which she presumed for Aimee and one directly across from Rein. She mentally considered how satisfying it would be to kick him in the shins and added cowboy boots t her list of immediate purchases.

Wyatt and the others rose as she came around the table. Rein a little slower on the uptake. She'd never received that kind of treatment, even from Angelo. Aimee appeared from the kitchen, a glass of juice in hand. Liberty noticed her skin had a waxy, pale sheen to it. She sat down with a quiet sigh and dropped her napkin in her lap. At the opposite end of the table sat a man with similar facial features as Wyatt's, but with a different build. Where Wyatt was taller and slightly lanky, this man had broad shoulders that filled out his black tee shirt. He remained standing, his gaze narrowing on Liberty as he held out his hand.

"I'm Dalton. And you must be Liberty Belle." He had his brother's intensely brown eyes. "I apologize for not being here last night when you arrived. I had a previous engagement."

Wyatt shot his brother a dark look. Rein cleared his throat.

"Don't pay attention to them. They don't understand my passion for pool." Dalton grinned.

"Or for Dusty's Place in general," Wyatt mumbled. "Ow." He darted a glance at his fiancée, who apparently had worn her boots.

"Are you familiar with the game?" Dalton asked ignoring his brother's remark.

Liberty took his proffered hand, feeling an immediate camaraderie to Dalton. "I carry a Fury HL."

A low-whistle and raised brow from Dalton followed. His smile, as handsome as Wyatt's, indicted she'd already won him over. "A classic style. I'm impressed."

Liberty shrugged. "I spent a lot of time at the Riviera, watching the tournaments. You can't touch Kelly "Kwikfire" Fisher."

Dalton closed his eyes and slapped his hand to his heart. "A woman after my own heart. Maybe we can head up to Dusty's, and you can show me what you've got."

She nodded and sat down, grinning at him. Maybe things weren't going so be so bad after all. "I'd like that."

Rein shifted in his chair. "If you two wouldn't mind holding off on comparing pool cues, I'd like to go over what needs to be done before this ranch in inundated with people in a couple of days."

Dalton made a face and gave Liberty a conspirator-type wink.

"I would like to meet the person who brings new energy to this house," stated an older man seated next to Rein. His silver and black hair trailed down his back in a single braid. His face, weathered by years of being in the sun, appeared serene. In his eyes, there was an unmistakable wisdom.

Wyatt took Aimee's hand, respect clear in how he looked at the man. "Liberty, this is Michael Greyfeather. He's one of my dad's dearest friends and knows this ranch—hell, he knows this entire area better than any of us."

"It is an honor to meet you." The old man nodded.

"And this is Tyler Jacobs," Rein said. "He owns the heating and plumbing store in town." The man, probably close to Rein's age, nodded as he reached across and took Liberty's hand.

"Ma'am."

The odd mix of people impressed on Liberty how, despite their diversity, these people had come together as family. It gave her a glimmer of hope that she, too, might make a connection here.

"It's nice to meet you all, but please. Go on with your conversation. I'm anxious to hear more about these cabins."

Dalton dug into his breakfast, while Wyatt and Aimee seemed preoccupied in a quiet conversation. Mr. Greyfeather spoke up, "It is Rein who's best suited to explain his uncle's vision. It's a journey we all walk, but he is leading us."

Remembering what Aimee said the night before, she wanted to learn more. "I'd very much like to hear about your uncle's dream." Liberty started in on her breakfast, beginning to feel a connection to those around her.

"Jed believed in hard work, thought it made a person stronger. God knows, that's how he raised the three of us. He had a giving way about him, always doing for others and very involved in the community. He decided one day, he'd like to make the ranch a place where folks without direction could, through work and nature, find purpose and perhaps a sense of direction in their lives."

Liberty listened, heat flushing her face as she realized that he could have been talking about her. She glanced up and caught his steady gaze, realizing that to him, she was a test run...a guinea pig in need of reformation. She averted her eyes from his by pushing around the food on her plate. "It sounds like a noble undertaking. Maybe I can be of some help?"

Rein drained the last of his coffee and cleared his throat. "I've got Dalton, thanks." He dismissed her offer and turned to Aimee. "What time did you say Sally'd be by?"

Aimee's gaze turned to Rein, and then scanned the faces

around the table. Her mouth turned down. Her expression wavered between panic and confusion as she slapped her hand to her mouth and darted from the table. From the bathroom nearby, came sounds that had the rugged men at the table pushing back their plates. Their faces silently questioning if the others understood what had just happened.

Liberty looked from one to the other. "When is the wedding?"

"This Sunday afternoon." Dalton answered. Wyatt fidgeted with his fork, uncertain whether to go to Aimee's aid or not. There was no way of escaping the horrid sounds echoing from the bathroom.

Liberty picked up her coffee cup and glanced at Wyatt. "It's a good thing, because that lady's got a great deal more going on." The dark circles, the emotions, and the smell of fried food...it became as clear as a wide Montana sky.

Wyatt's gaze turned to her. "Like what?" Rein and Dalton asked in unison with their older brother.

"Like a baby." She stared at their blank collective gaze. "Really? You didn't notice the symptoms?"

The shock registered on Wyatt's face was answer enough.

CB

With all the chaos going on with preparation for the wedding, now the bride-to-be puked up her guts on a regular basis. Rein watched Liberty step in without being asked, to take care of things like preparing meals and cleaning the kitchen. He and Dalton on the other hand, tried to stay away from the main house as much as possible. Rein woke at dawn, determined to finish the cabin before the weekend

The insistent ring of his cell phone prompted him to search for the device hidden beneath the sheets of blueprints. He grabbed the phone and punched to answer the familiar number. "What's up, Hank?" The caller, Henry "Hank" Richardson, a close friend and old college classmate, who now lived now in Illinois. When he found out that Hank received his pilot's license, the Kinnison ranch hired him to fly them regularly to meetings with buyers. Last December the three—Dalton, Rein and Hank—found themselves grounded when an unexpected blizzard swept across the Dakotas and Iowa. The same storm had left Aimee and a small group of her students stranded at the ranch while on a field trip. While Wyatt revealed little in the way of details of that three-day confinement, it was clear that the experience had left him a changed man.

By New Year's Eve he'd proposed to Aimee, and they began plans to marry at the ranch come late spring. It was a welcome change that set a renewed interest in just about everything in Wyatt's once solitary existence, including a major financial push toward building the cabins to fulfill Jed Kinnison's dream of making Last Hope Ranch a place to heal.

"Hey, just wanted to give you a buzz and ask if it'd be okay to bring Caroline with me this weekend. She's back from Europe for a visit and has been asking about you."

Caroline. His gut clenched with the sound of her name. Hank's little sister. He'd met her the first time he'd gone home with Hank for a weekend. He'd been her first, on a rainy day in the privacy of the pool house on the Richardson estate. To his knowledge, no one, not even Hank at the time, had known. When she started the next fall at the same college, they had resumed their intense affair, barely leaving each other's side for the next three years. Rein was smitten, certain she would be the only woman he could ever love. He'd prepared to propose to her when she received the opportunity to go study abroad in her last semester. Promises made. Passionate declarations and weekly letters followed for a time. But after a month, the letters waned, and the relationship eventually grew cold. It had been a bittersweet split, and Hank had enough sensitivity not to bring up his sister's name when he and Rein were together. "Caroline?" Her name rolled of his tongue in quiet reverence.

"Yeah, my little sister?" There was a pause on the line. "She saw the invitation and wanted me to ask if you'd mind her tagging along. She wanted to see how you're doing. Catch up."

Rein blinked from the memory of the statuesque dark-haired beauty that dominated nearly his every waking moment and most of his dreams. *Catch up?* "Things are a little crazy, Hank. I'm up to my armpits in this cabin rental project."

"Yeah, I told her about your furniture-making skills. She mentioned that she'd like to see your work." Rein hesitated, unsure how he'd feel seeing her again.

"Hey, I realize that you two kind of had a thing once. If it's too uncomfortable, I'll tell her. I'm sure she'll understand."

Rein chewed the corner of his lip. *A thing?* Yeah, it was damn lucky she hadn't gotten pregnant—kind of *thing*. But Hank didn't know that. Few did. It had been explosive. They were young, taking risks, living for the moment and not caring about anyone else. *A thing?* Hell, yeah. Would it be setting off a powder keg to see her again? Maybe, maybe not. Had she gotten married? Did she have kids? His curiosity made him want to drill Hank for more information, but at the same time, the memory of his affair with Caroline had taken a long time to shake off. Unsure of what seeing her again might dredge up, he'd just have to 'cowboy up' and find out. "Sure, bring her along. It'll be great to see her." He played down the remark as he smoothed his thumb along a sheet of bubble wrap packing and then wadded it in his fist, feeling the small pockets burst in succession beneath his grasp.

"Great, we'll fly into End of the Line and call you Friday night. Any plans to throw Wyatt a bachelor party?"

Rein raised his brows. "Uh, nope. Wyatt told us he preferred to have a family dinner this week and invite the attendants, so that's what we're doing. That's about as crazy as Wyatt wants things just now." He didn't feel it necessary to explain between the wedding and getting used to the idea of being a dad, his brother had enough crazy going on in his life.

"Fair enough. See you soon then, buddy."

"Okay, Hank. Safe travel." He broke off the connection and stared at the wad of bubble wrap in his fist. Dalton had gone out to chop up some wood to bring in for the stove. Even though late spring, the mountains still got chilly at night. He heard a loud thump and his head jerked up. Liberty, who'd dropped her giant duffle bag, stood inside the front door, her gaze scanning the interior of the cabin.

Rein frowned. "What are you doing here?" He hadn't meant for the comment to come out quite so brusque. She ignored his blunt remark and continued to look around the room.

"Aimee's folks just arrived. I thought they should stay up at the house. They're her family and besides, Aimee might like some private time with her mom."

June and Ward Worth were delightful people, full of fun and a true testament to the sanctity of marriage. They'd come for a brief visit early on in the engagement and fell into sync quickly with the ranch, the town, and Wyatt. You couldn't ask for better in-laws. They'd lost their other daughter—Aimee's twin—in a tragic car accident. That alone bonded Rein to Aimee in a way that only those suffering such a loss could understand. In honor of her sister's dream to teach in an area of greatest need, Aimee relocated to End of the Line.

"Besides, the maid of honor, Sally, has shown up every morning since she learned of Aimee's condition. I figure even if the cabin's only partway done, I can make do. I feel sort of in the way up there."

That, he couldn't fault her for. He'd felt the same way after Aimee started staying there. Rein scratched the nape of his neck. A back up in orders had caused a delay in finalizing the plumbing in the other cabin, so he and Dalton decided to bunk in Liberty's future cabin. He hadn't anticipated Aimee's sudden bout of morning sickness that occurred at all times of the day or night. He hadn't anticipated news of Caroline showing up, or Liberty choosing to stay elsewhere. He released an audible sigh. This wasn't how he preferred things to go. He liked organization. He liked schedules.

"I suppose Dalton and I can bunk at the other cabin for a few days. We'll just have to shower and use the facilities in the main house."

She folded her arms over her chest and tipped her head. "Why would you have to do that?"

Rein forced his gaze from her tanned cleavage and pretended he hadn't been debating whether or not she wore a bra. He averted his eyes, blaming his wayward thoughts on Caroline. Liberty, however, was as close to a little sister as he'd ever get. He needed to get his perspective straight, right quick. "I'm sorry, come again?"

Her brows disappeared beneath the blue striped bangs she wore this morning. "Excuse me?"

Realizing she wasn't familiar with his comment, he explained. "I need you to repeat what you said, I didn't hear you."

"Oh." She dropped her arms and sauntered past him, running her hand over the cabinets he'd built. "Come again. It sounds like something else, *entirely*." She glanced his way and smiled. "I suppose that's the difference between city girls and country boys."

He shifted, feeling embarrassed to be having this conversation with Dalton's little sister, when he might walk in at any moment.

"What I meant to say, is you shouldn't have to tromp all the way up to the main house. If the other cabin is close to this one, we can set up a bathroom schedule. I'm used to sharing with roommates. Besides, I normally shower at night. But we won't go into that." She opened the refrigerator, spotted a longneck beer and held it up. "Do you mind?"

Rein was still processing the whole "sharing the bathroom" idea. "Uh sure, go ahead."

She twisted off the cap and lifted herself to sit on the counter. Taking a drink, she glanced his way and raised a brow. "What do you think?"

Of your thin cami top, or your jeans with enough holes to leave damn little to the imagination? Rein opened his mouth to speak, just as Dalton stepped through the patio screen door. "Hey, Liberty. See you found sanctuary. The only thing worse than a man puking his guts up, is the sound of a woman retching."

"You have poetic tendencies, Dalton." She lifted her bottle in salute and took another swallow. "I told Rein that Aimee's folks arrived, and I decided to move out to give them Rein's room."

"Hey, there's always my room." Dalton shrugged, dropping the wood by the stove.

"Have you looked at your room?" Rein and Liberty blurted the words together as if on cue. Liberty's unbridled laughter caused Rein's mouth to lift in a smile.

She took another swallow from the bottle. "Besides, once they shovel out your room, Dalton, the wedding party is going to need the space to get ready. I figure it's easier on everyone this way."

Dalton reached into the fridge and snagged himself a beer. He held it up and tapped Liberty's bottle. "Fine by me. We can make this work. Rein and I will just head down to the next cabin." He took a swig from the bottle and then frowned. "Except that we have no plumbing."

"Which is where you came in," Rein sighed, still contemplating the options.

"I suggested a bathroom schedule." Liberty spoke directly to Dalton.

A grin spread across his face. "Perfect. It's settled. I'll go get the truck and we'll load up some of the furniture that's going into the cabin."

"I'll help." Liberty hopped off the counter and followed Dalton out the door.

Clearly, they'd not waited to hear his thoughts on the subject. Rein squeezed the tired piece of plastic in his fist and tossed it in the trash. When had he lost control? A sobering thought occurred to him. The last time his life went topsy-turvy, was when Caroline Richardson waltzed into it.

And look how that turned out.

In theory, this should be the happiest week of his older brother's life. So why did he feel like a bad moon was rising?

Chapter Four

*E*verything seemed to be coming together. Liberty had never seen such a large group work so cohesively to make something happen. She stood on the front porch, a cup of coffee in hand and watched as Rein, Dalton, and Michael followed Sally's orders, relieved that she'd been given charge over Aimee. Wyatt took refuge inside with a couple of others from town, storing the bales of hay in the upper floor of the barn.

"Did we remember the ladders? I've got to get up there to drape the rafters with the tulle." She called after the men struggling to carry two eight-foot banquet tables at a time.

The Church of Christ had allowed them to borrow a few for the reception. The horses had been regulated to the pens outside, the barn floor was in process of being swept and bales of hay with blankets donated by Michael and Rebecca had been placed around the barn inside and outside, for extra seating. A small stage for a local country band had been arranged at one end of the building. Seating for two hundred, Aimee had told her, meant that she'd nearly invited the entire town, in addition to an array of out of town family, clients and friends.

Aimee, who'd slept in a little later these past couple of mornings, appeared at Liberty's side, looking pleasantly tired.

"Morning," she commented in lackluster fashion.

The two stood in silence a moment watching the male energy and Sally's teaching skills in action.

"She's a force to be reckoned with," Liberty remarked. She genuinely liked Sally and it appeared she got along well with Rein.

"She's a teacher," Aimee responded as she settled into one of the porches four hand-made rocking chairs. Liberty chose to stand.

"Is there a story between those two?" She glanced back and caught Aimee's puzzled frown.

"What two?"

Liberty tipped her head toward Rein and Sally. She was speaking to him and his focus didn't waver.

"You mean, Sally and Rein?

"Are they an item." She crooked two fingers of her free hand into quotes to emphasize. "He seems very tuned into to her."

She heard Aimee's short laugh. "Wow, you noticed that?"

Liberty gave her a side-look. "I know men."

Aimee could have used the comment to make a seedy remark, but Liberty noticed she didn't. In the short time she'd known her, Liberty realized that Aimee held few judgments about people—unlike others around here.

Her gaze shot back to Rein. Head down, he trudged from the barn, his hat shading his face from view. A man with a mission—determined—a no-nonsense kind of guy. His boots roused the dirt as he stomped toward the truck. He paused a moment to remove his hat and wipe his brow with his forearm. She noted the ripple of solid muscle beneath his gray cotton tee shirt. His snap up, long-sleeve shirt lay in a wad beneath a tree where he'd tossed it.

"Any particular reason that you're interested?"

Aimee's gentle voice interrupted her thoughts. She faced her new friend and leaned against the railing, purposely turning her back on Rein. "Just curious. He seems to get along with her."

Aimee nodded with a quiet smile. "And he hasn't been very kind to you, has he?"

Liberty shrugged. "I'm a big girl, Aimee. I've seen plenty in my twenty-one years. I've never had anyone treat me like I'm twelve before. Especially a man."

Aimee studied her a moment before she spoke, "I heard that they dated a while back. Long before I moved here. I also heard it didn't work out. Rein's not at all Sally's type. And truth be told, I think Sally would have killed him eventually."

Why that should give her a spark of satisfaction, she didn't understand, but didn't plan to go there, just yet. Besides, he hadn't shown any interest in even getting to know her as a friend. "Maybe he thinks I'm a threat to his brothers?"

"Why would he think that?"

"Aimee," she smiled. "In my line of work, you don't need to know someone well...hell, at all, before jumping to all kinds of ridiculous conclusions."

"Give him time. He'll come around."

She wouldn't hold her breath. A woman's laugh caught her attention and she looked back to see Rein and Sally in an animated conversation. Envy nibbled at her, and she shouldn't give a red hot damn. No doubt she found him physically attractive, but they had little else in common, other than their love of interior design. And even in that, he didn't seem interested in her opinions.

"Have you thought about what you're going to wear to the wedding?"

Liberty eyed the pert blonde woman, her hair askew, looking groggy in her bathrobe and white flip-flops—and still beautiful. Liberty sighed.

"Not until this moment. I didn't bring a lot with me in the way of dress clothes."

Aimee's brow furrowed. "You left your things back in Vegas? Were you thinking that you might be going back?"

"Uh, no. I was sort of in a hurry."

Aimee stood and stuffed her hands in the pockets of the

blue plaid robe. The way it hung on her, Liberty figured it had to be Wyatt's. "Liberty. Are you in trouble?"

She searched the petite woman's eyes filled with concern. Aimee had enough on her plate this week. "No, of course not." It wasn't a complete lie. As long as Angelo was appeased by the letter that she'd quit and broken her contract with him. "You know that if you need anything, need someone to talk you, you can come to me."

Liberty smiled and drained the cup of now cold coffee. "Sure. I just need a little time to figure out what's next for me. Maybe I could find work in something I really want to do."

"Which is?"

"Design. Interiors. Color, fabric, textures. I love working with that stuff."

Aimee offered a friendly smile. "Well listen, in the meantime, why don't you come inside and let's take a look in my closet. I think I've got a dress that will fit you perfectly."

The unexpected sense of belonging hit Liberty hard. She rubbed her hand under her nose and blinked a couple of times to clear the haze of tears threatening to spill over. "Remind me please to take my allergy meds. All this nature is playing havoc on me."

Aimee laughed and gestured for her to follow. With a quick look over her shoulder, she noticed Rein alone, pulling another table off the back of the truck. His gaze connected to hers and heat slammed into her.

Damn.

A few moments later, she watched Aimee rifle through her closet in a quest to find something she felt Liberty could wear. "Ah, here it is. This one ought to catch his eye." She pulled out a deep purple-colored short dress, made of a shimmery satin fabric. It was sleeveless with a single strap over one shoulder. Liberty eyed the gorgeous dress as she plucked it from Aimee's hands.

"I have no idea what you're talking about, but this is a gorgeous dress."

A pair of sparkling blue eyes peeked around the garment. "Really? You forget I am used to having a sister. I know the signs."

"Signs? Please." She ducked her gaze and laid the dress on the bed. Liberty began to pull off her clothes as Aimee sauntered to the window and pulled shut the curtains to the side porch door. She settled in an easy chair in the corner of the room and rested her chin on her hand.

"How long have you had that blue streak in your hair?"

Liberty released a small sigh and slid the zipper down the side of the dress. "A few months. It looks good in my dark hair, don't you think?" She blatantly tested Aimee's curiosity, wondering whether Aimee's acceptance of her was sincere.

"Yeah," The woman's response seemed lukewarm.

"Yeah?"

"And the tongue piercing?"

"My boss's idea. He thought it made the dancers look exotic. It hurt like hell."

"Why don't you take it out?" she asked.

Liberty let the beautiful dress slither down over her body. It fit as though designed for her. "You might not like the answer."

Aimee chuckled. "I'm not that backwoods, Liberty. Is it better for guys or gals?"

She spun on her heel, surprised that a second grade teacher would be so blunt. "First, let's be clear. I'm into men. If that's what you're wondering. And I guess I've heard that guys don't seem to mind it." She grinned and they both broke into laughter.

"For the record, I like the hair. I once thought about putting a pink streak in my hair, but chickened out. Yeah, I admit it." She tipped her head thoughtfully. "You know, you look a whole lot better in that dress than I ever did. I might have to hate you a little. As to the piercing...I say whatever works. Besides, there are a couple of good-looking cowboys around town. You never know." She wiggled her brows.

"Now you're trying to set me up?"

"Me?" Aimee smiled.

"You hardly know me, Aimee. And if I go by Wyatt's reaction to me the night I got here or Rein's constant advice—my, God, I don't think he knows how to categorize me. The sense I'm getting is that not to many of those "cowboys" in town, are going to come flocking to me."

"Liberty, around here, a change in Betty's breakfast menu can cause a stir in town. Don't worry about the opinion of others. Once they get to know you, they'll warm up." Aimee smiled. "I can remember when people didn't think that Wyatt could ever change from the sullen hermit he used to be. The townsfolk called him, The Grinch."

"Wyatt, a Grinch? Preposterous." She grinned and Aimee shrugged.

"I guess part of me likes to think that maybe I had something to do with the change in his demeanor. Ultimately, Wyatt had to realize there was more to him than he allowed himself to be."

"He's still a little tightly wrapped around the edges, but he seems happy. Love must agree with him."

"It can be a powerful thing." She eyed Liberty. "Are *you* happy with the way you look?"

Liberty walked over to the dresser mirror and gazed at her reflection. In the short time she'd been at the ranch, she felt more rested. Even her skin glowed. The color of the dress and the style suited her athletic build. She eyed it, figuring with the right heels and hairstyle, Rein MacKenzie would be convinced that she wasn't the little girl he thought her to be.

☙

Thank God they'd thought to install the cattle fans in the rafters. Even with both doors open at either end of the barn, the fancy jacket was too hot for Rein. Just as soon as they cut the cake and the traditional toasts were made, he wasted no time crawling out of the black tuxedo jacket, unbuttoning his collar, and rolling up the sleeves on his dress shirt.

"I'm going to get some of Betty's lemonade. You want anything?" He clapped Dalton on the shoulder. His brother eased back in his chair, nursing a beer as he quietly observed the celebration in front of him. The entire town had practically turned out for the reception after the family and friends ceremony.

"No, I'm good." He didn't look up.

"You okay, man?" Rein stood next to his brother's chair. Dalton had been unusually quiet since the ceremony. His toast to the new couple had been simple, straightforward. Then again, Dalton wasn't necessarily a sentimental guy.

"It's just weird to think of him being married, you know? And me, going to be an uncle."

Rein slapped his hand on Dalton's shoulder. "Hey, we're all getting older, bro."

"Yeah, I just hope they make it."

Words that came from a past so much different than Rein's. His parents had their moments, sure, but they loved each other. They were a family. Rein had to live with what had been taken from him every day. He took a deep breath, forcing away the complicated memory on this otherwise happy day. "They will, Dal and you'll make a damn fine uncle, you'll see." His brother nodded and clasped Rein's hand briefly.

A few moments later, Rein stood at the refreshment table with a glass of Betty's homemade special brew in hand. He took in the sight around him, the soft white tulle and sparkling tiny white lights in the rafters, the electric pillar candles in mason jars on the tables. Sally had really come through in transforming the old barn into a wedding night to remember. His gaze caught Wyatt and Aimee nose-to-nose on the dance floor, wrapped in an intimate embrace. He'd never seen Wyatt so happy. It was about damn time.

"Hey, cowboy, how about you take this dress out for a spin. I want to get as much use out of it as possible." Sally tapped his shoulder and smiled up at him. He set down his empty glass, and led her to the dance floor. The music and the spiked lemonade slipped through his veins. He sighed and looked down at Sally. "You did an incredible job with all this, lady."

"Why thank you, sir. Anything for those two, right?" She looked at the newlyweds, oblivious to anyone else in the room "Have you ever seen Wyatt smile so much?"

"I know. I've never seen him like this."

"About damn time." They both said at once and then laughed. It was strange at times being around Sally. They'd shared a brief, but not an intimate, past. Rein had on more than one occasion, wondered why. Tonight however, his mind wandered aimlessly, jumping from one thought to another, and more often than not, landing on Liberty.

"Liberty certainly seems like a nice girl."

Rein's gaze darted to hers. Had she read his mind? The comment came so fast and unexpected that it rattled him for a moment. "Yeah, for a kid."

A smile curled the corner of Sally's lip.

"What's with the smirk?"

She raised her brow. "Well, first off, she's of age, which means she's no kid, as you put it. And honey, you didn't take your eyes off of her during the entire ceremony."

"You're reading into things," he stated flatly, averting his eyes. He knew she was spot on with her observation. He'd not been able to keep his brain focused on much else since she walked across the lawn in that dress. All afternoon he'd been battling his wayward thoughts about Liberty.

Sally tapped his shoulder. "Oh, look. Angelique is talking to Dalton."

Grateful at least, that they'd changed the topic, he twirled Sally, so he could see Dalton's reaction. Never mind that it might have given him the chance to search that side of the room for Liberty.

"Would you look at that slug." She craned her head to look over her shoulder and released a frustrated sigh. "He could have at least asked her to dance."

"Dalton doesn't dance."

"Well, he ought to learn."

Rein grinned down at her. "Forever the optimist."

"What is it going to take for a girl to win that guy's heart?"

Rein blinked, drawing back in genuine surprise. "Wait a second, are you interested in Dalton?"

Indignation flashed in her wide green eyes. "Hell, no. Dating one of you was *plenty* for me."

"Hey, it wasn't so bad."

She glanced up at him and smiled. "Not bad, just not right."

He nodded and wondered if Sally ever pondered why it hadn't worked between them. Not until Sally had ended the relationship and they had chosen to remain friends, did Rein realize he'd started dating her in a rebound move after Caroline left him. Though they did have fun together, at the time when it would have been natural for the relationship to progress to the next level, neither felt the spark between them that ought to be there.

He studied the scene, watching Michael Greyfeather's niece attempt to engage Dalton in a conversation. The poor thing had no idea that given his mood, getting him to speak at all was akin to talking to a mule. His body language. On the other hand, spoke volumes—arms crossed, staring straight ahead-a proverbial, immovable force not to be reckoned with. "In answer to your question. Maybe a two-by-four?"

Sally's laughter filtered through the music as their dance ended.

"I'm parched." He nodded toward the refreshment table. "Betty's got her special homemade lemonade over there. Can I get you some?"

"I'm good, thank you. Think I'll go talk to Angelique. She might need an ear to vent to after that little display of wills. I bet he doesn't even remember her. She used to have a wicked crush on him."

Rein blinked in surprise. He remembered her as a shy girl with long dark hair and knew that back in middle school she'd had to move away with her mother after a scandalous divorce. "I heard Michael telling Wyatt that things haven't been easy for her. Apparently, that's why Emily was under their guardianship."

Sally nodded. "She's been through a ton of crap, Rein. You wouldn't believe it. And it started with her mom. But this isn't the time or place for such talk and besides, I'm not sure that Angelique is ready to make what she's been through public knowledge, you know?"

Rein understood. He had some things he'd never shared with anyone but his brothers. He glanced again at Dalton. No, he wouldn't have noticed her in school. She wasn't his type, and apparently still wasn't, but that didn't make him discerning, just a fool, because she'd grown up to be a fine-looking woman.

The unfortunate truth, Rein thought reluctantly was that Dalton hadn't changed much since high school. He still considered himself a free spirit, loved having a good time, and wasn't ready yet to be tied down. The woman who broke through the wall he'd slapped up to defend the pain of his past, would have to possess strength to match his will. Sensing Sally's concern, however, he offered to speak to Dalton. "You want me to say something to him?"

"Nah, but I do like that two-by-four idea." She pushed up on her toes and kissed his cheek. "We're a couple of fine examples to talk about relationships, aren't we?" He saw a flash of melancholy in her smile.

"Sally, I...."

She furrowed her brow and touched her finger to his lips. "Stop. You drove me crazy, you still do, but that's another story. The *real* story is that there is this incredible woman standing over by the cake table that hasn't stopped looking at you since we started dancing. Do you know her?"

Rein followed Sally's gaze and met Caroline's happy

expression. She gave him a jaunty wave. "That would be, Caroline Richardson."

"Really? Is she related to Hank?"

"His sister." Rein waited for Sally's reaction.

"Oh, *that* Caroline."

"Yep." He tossed Sally a side-look. "And I'd appreciate you not saying anything more. She asked to come with Hank. No one invited her."

"Interesting though, you have to admit." She offered an ornery grin.

Rein sighed and leaned forward to press a soft kiss on her forehead. "See you later." He watched her walk away, grateful for her friendship. He cleared his throat, and prepared to speak to Caroline, deciding he couldn't avoid her all night. Her smile welcomed him. She opened her arms and drew him close, kissing him European fashion on both cheeks. Despite the fact of standing in a horse-barn, she smelled exotic, still wearing that sweet French perfume she always wore.

"Darling, How are you? I'm so sorry we're late. There was a problem with a flap or some wing gadget, and it caused a delay. We snuck in just in time to see you lift the bride up behind Wyatt on his horse and ride off into the sunset." She clasped her hands under her chin. "So, utterly romantic in a small town, sort of way." She took a step back in approving assessment, stepping forward to brush invisible lint from his shirt. "And you look particularly handsome tonight, Mr. Mackenzie

Rein's cheeks warmed. That damn well didn't happen often. He'd hoped she'd forgotten how easily she could push his buttons, but it appeared she still had her touch.

"You're looking well, Caroline." He hadn't expected that seeing her again would prove to be so awkward. He hadn't really been sure what to expect. He eyed the refreshment table with its country-themed motif. "Have you tried this lemonade? Betty, she owns the diner in town and has," he stepped around her as he spoke, "pretty much catered this whole affair tonight." He surveyed the number of mixer choices and spotting the Jack Daniels, filled a blue mason jar with equal parts of both. He offered the same to Caroline. Her face puckered and she shook her head.

"Plain for me, thanks. Unless it's good champagne. You know me and flying."

"Oh, so you guys have to take off tonight?" Rein kept his eyes on his task, trying not to sound too anxious for her to leave, even though it was true. He caught the sight of Liberty a few feet away, offering to take a tray of dirty dishes from Betty. Despite the fact that he found her choices on some things to be odd, if not downright strange, it appeared she could hold her own and had an impressive work ethic. She didn't mind stepping in to help, and she seemed to be fitting in well with her new-found family. Regardless of how busy he'd been this week, he'd taken notice of how well she'd adapted and concluded intellectually that it was the influence of his uncle's vision that had given him such clarity.

"That one certainly isn't from around here, is she?"

Rein hadn't realized he'd been staring. He pulled from his reverie and handed Caroline her drink. "That's Wyatt and Dalton's half-sister." He took a healthy swallow from his glass. "Her name's Liberty."

"You're serious?" She gave him an incredulous look. "As in the Liberty Bell?"

Rein shrugged, wishing to avoid any conversation directly related to Liberty.

Caroline's gaze was demure as she took a sip of her drink. "Strange name to give a child. Cute though. I suppose if you find that horrid Goth look at all attractive."

A sweet buzz had taken over Rein's brain. Probably not a good thing. "What's a Goth look like, exactly?" Her snobbish attitude got to him, or maybe her perfume, then again, maybe it was the memory of how they were in bed. Whatever the reason, he felt edgy, restless and not up for Caroline's verbal dissection of anyone from his life. She'd done that once before, only he hadn't been smart enough to see it until they'd broken up.

She issued a condescending chuckle. "You still don't get out much, do you?"

Apparently, her critical opinion of his rural lifestyle hadn't changed. She'd never understood his purpose here at the ranch as anything but an inability to leave his "hick" town. "Why don't you enlighten me, Caroline?" He took another sip to fortify his gentlemanly manners.

Oblivious to his pointed remark, she gingerly took a sip from the jar, looking awkwardly uncomfortable. Rein realized suddenly just how out of place she must feel and yet, had no real sympathy for her. He waited, anticipating the sharp scalpel of her tongue.

"Well, for starters, she's wearing that heavy make-up, the first sign that she is not a conformist to proper societal protocol." Caroline assessed Liberty from afar as though she was a professional in profiling.

Clearly, the woman had never bothered to do a self-evaluation. Rein gulped down half his jar, each moment becoming increasingly aware that Caroline had no thought to keep her voice down.

"And oh-my-god, that odd blue streak in her hair? Really? And did you notice that tattoo on her shoulder? Come on, she might have at least tried for the sake of her brother's wedding to use a little cover up. It just shows she has no regard for family."

He couldn't remember anyone in the family making any comments about covering up any tattoo. "Tattoo?" He acted as though he hadn't noticed, even though he must have traced it mentally a hundred times as he sat at the head table during supper and watched Liberty interact with Betty and her husband.

"I'd keep a close eye on her. Those people can get caught up in some strange things. Covens, sacrifices, even violence, so I've heard. And now with Aimee and the baby, well...." She took another drink. "I'm guessing that you'll all sleep a little easier after she's gone."

Rein listened, grateful for the whiskey gliding down his parched throat. East coast conservative upbringing aside, Caroline had gotten on his last nerve. "Yeah, well." He slammed the glass on the table and pinned Caroline with a steady look. "I don't think there's much to be concerned about. She's a good kid."

Caroline tipped her head and raised one perfect brow. "She doesn't exactly look like any kid I know. How old do you suppose she is, anyway?"

Why the sudden interest in Liberty tonight? Hell, she was barely out of her teens, but possessed the body of a full-grown woman. "Um, you know, I'm not really sure and frankly, why do you care?" He tipped his head and looked at her. "So what do you say? A dance for old-time's sake?" He didn't wait for her response, but grabbed the drink and her hand, dragging her to the dance floor. He wanted...no he needed to talk about something other than Liberty. The fact that she appeared in his mind too often these days made him uncomfortable.

"Well," she spoke in a flustered, southern-belle voice. "I guess we'll dance." From the open doors, he saw the last dredges of the sunset casting long shadows across the mountains.

"Penny for your thoughts." Caroline's voice jarred him from his reverie.

He searched her beautiful eyes, asking himself how he never seen past her façade. "I'm just thinking how damn lucky I am to live here."

The realization that he'd put her ideas about the ranch not being worth much in her place, panned across her face.

"I never said it wasn't beautiful, Rein." He heard the note of tension in her voice.

He offered a congenial smile. "No, you didn't. But it still isn't beautiful *enough* for you, is it?"

"Rein, I—"

He shook his head and took a step back. "It's okay, Caroline. I understand you needed more, but I'm okay with how things turned out. I wouldn't have wanted you to stay where you weren't content." By the look on her face, he guessed that she might not be content anywhere, no matter how beautiful. Not until she could be content in her own skin. The realization created a stark contrast in his mind between her and Liberty. Despite their differences, he should have defended Liberty against her barbed comments. Had it been Dalton she'd spoken ill of, he'd never tolerated it. Liberty was kin to the two men that had treated him as a blood brother from the time he came to live with them after the car accident that claimed his parents, leaving him an orphan. His Uncle Jed had taken him in without hesitation. How could he not at least show the same consideration for this young girl? He had the sudden urgent need to make things right with her.

Her expression appeared puzzled. "Are you implying I'm not content?"

Rein shrugged. "That's something only you can answer, Caroline." He carefully motioned to Dalton to relieve him on the dance floor. His brother shook his head. He didn't like Caroline any more than the rest of his family did. Rein gave him a look that would kill and Dalton relented with a scowl.

"May I cut in?" He shot Rein a dark look before Caroline saw the exchange.

"Hey, Dalton." He acted surprised. "Caroline, you remember my brother, Dalton?" He stepped away from Caroline and offered his spot to his less than thrilled brother. Dalton stepped around him, leaning close in Rein's earshot. "You owe me," he whispered. And then, with a bright smile, held his arms out to Caroline.

"Hey Caroline, welcome back to the backwoods. You had any of Betty's possum pie?"

Rein hid a smile. He'd owe him...big time. Dalton's tolerance of Caroline's attitude was far less than his and for a brief moment, he felt guilty leaving her at his mercy. But it didn't last long.

"Listen, if you two will excuse me. I need to check on something." Rein looked at Caroline. "If I don't get the chance to see you off, have a safe flight, and tell Hank I'll be in touch." He patted his brother on the shoulder. Caroline's mouth was still gaped open when he left.

Stepping out of the barn, he noticed small clusters of guests enjoying the beautiful spring evening, but he saw no sign of Liberty. Was it wise to try to find her, or should he leave well enough alone? What were the odds she'd heard a word that Caroline said? Then again, Caroline's voice seemed to have turned heads of several folks standing nearby. He looked up and saw Betty walking down the lane from the main house. She carried a fresh pie in each hand. "Need any help?" He looked over her shoulder and wondered if Liberty might be close behind.

"Thanks, honey. I'm getting these to send home with Hank. You know how he likes my cherry pie."

"Yep, he loves them." He cast a quick look over her shoulder again. "You haven't seen Liberty around, have you?"

"Now that's funny. Wyatt just asked me the same thing."

Rein turned his focus on her then. "And?"

"Oh, I'd sent her to check on the buffet table to see if we needed more lemonade. She mentioned that you were in a very animated conversation with a lovely woman."

"Caroline Richardson."

Betty's jovial expression sobered. "Oh, I heard she was here. Liberty seemed a trifle upset."

Shit. She'd heard the scathing comments. He knew it in his gut. Rein released a heavy sigh. "I'm afraid Caroline said some things, and it sounds like Liberty might have overheard her." *And I did little to defend her.* "Did you see where she went?"

Betty tipped her head toward the main house. "Last I knew, she was up at the house, helping Wyatt put together some concoction to help Aimee's queasiness."

"Thanks, Betty."

"You're welcome." She started on down the lane and stopped. "Rein?"

He rolled his eyes, not figuring she'd let him off that easy. Betty had her opinions and often would share them, like it or not. "That Caroline."

"Yes, what about her, Betty?"

"Is she still full of herself, like I remember? Not that she ever set foot out here very often. Never really fit in, as I recall."

"Point taken, Betty."

"And one more thing."

"Uh huh."

"I think you should stop being so hard on Liberty. She's a good girl deep down under all that stuff she hides behind."

"Maybe she's not hiding at all, Betty. Maybe that's just who she is." Rein marveled at his comment, defending this woman against the very thoughts he'd been fighting for the past week.

Betty's smile shimmered like a Cheshire cat in the shadows. "Well now, that's a switch. I take it you didn't completely agree with Caroline's assessment?"

He was treading on shaky ground. Caroline had hurt him, and he'd survived it. But, he hadn't realized how cruel she could be to others until tonight. While Liberty's lifestyle choices were not his, Caroline had no right to speak as she had. "She doesn't always think before she speaks. It appears all her European travels haven't changed her much. She's still a snob. I just never realized how very different she and Hank are in their personalities."

Betty tipped her head. "Sounds like you care more than just a passing interest in how Liberty feels."

Rein shook his head, exasperated by the notion that everyone seemed bent on throwing him together with this young woman. "I just want to make sure she knows that Caroline can be insensitive and everyone knows it. Besides, Betty. She's just a kid." God knows he'd been trying to convince himself of that fact even as he fantasized what she might be wearing under that form-fitting dress.

"Not in that dress, she isn't." Betty laughed as though reading his mind. "Good luck with that." She continued on, her laughter taunting him as he headed to the main house.

He ran into Wyatt coming out the front door. He had one of the thermos bottles they normally took on cattle drives in his hand

"Hey." Wyatt stomped across the porch in his polished boots.

"Hey" Rein paused, his hand on the railing.

"Aimee felt queasy. She had Liberty mix up this stuff that she swears is a wonder drink for morning sickness. Seems as though Aimee has these bouts of sickness both day and night. Doc says its normal, but it bothers the hell out of me."

"It's been a long week. Doc also told her not to overdo, and if I know Aimee, she didn't listen. It'll get better once you guys get away for a few days alone."

Wyatt tromped down the steps. He slapped Rein on the shoulder. "Thanks. I'm looking forward to this wedding stuff being over and getting on with our life."

"Yeah, listen, is Liberty still inside?"

Wyatt stopped in his tracks and looked at Rein. "She said she'd be down in a few minutes. Now that I think about it, she seemed a little, I don't know...upset about something. She didn't appear to want to discuss it with me."

"Yeah." Rein looked at the ground.

"You know something about this?"

Wyatt took a step back toward him and rested his foot on the bottom step.

Rein scratched the back of his neck. "Maybe. I think she might have overheard some of the conversation between me and Caroline."

"Hank's sister? The snooty one who wanted you to go to Europe? The one we all thought you were going to marry?"

"One in the same. Hank brought her. She wanted to see me."

Wyatt raised his dark brows. "Is she still pretty?"

"Yeah, and just as snooty. Guess maybe I didn't see that before."

Wyatt chuckled. "You had your head in the clouds, maybe up your butt, as I recall. You were oblivious to damn near everything except her. I always got the impression that she put herself a bit higher than the rest of us. Strange, Hank's never acted that way."

Rein nodded. "That's just it. I think it's all an act. The woman doesn't seem to be comfortable unless she's tearing down someone else. I think I might have dodged a bullet on that one." Rein gave his brother a guilty look. "I left her down there with Dalton."

"Oh shit. You didn't." Wyatt face broke into a wide smile. "I don't know which I'd find more interesting to watch, Dal with Miss Caroline, or you trying to appease Liberty's anger."

"Angry, you think she's angry?" God help him if there was a lick of truth to what Caroline said.

Wyatt offered him an ornery grin. "You may want to make sure she's put away the knife from cutting cucumbers, before you speak to her."

Chapter Five

*G*lad for a few moments to collect herself, Liberty hadn't anticipated how hearing a complete stranger pronounce such vicious judgments about her would cut so deeply. Added to the fact her comments had garnered the stares of several guests nearby as well. Thankfully, she snuck out the back door, and hurried to the main house without encountering any guests. It infuriated her that her thoughts about the gorgeous woman fawning all over Rein were just as distasteful.

The woman was a fake from her clothing, to her laugh, appearing to be better than everyone around her. Mostly, it killed her to think she would be the type to capture Rein's attention. Little Miss Perfect—too perfect, to Liberty's way of thinking. The kind of woman that only has to "want" something and it's given to her on a silver platter. And it appeared she wanted Rein. Her thoughtless manner, her hurtful words, had bruised her ego, but far worse, far more devastating a blow was Rein's toss-away response—

"She's a good kid."

She leaned her head on the back of the couch and released a sigh. What kind of futile game was she playing here? Did she really think that someone like Rein Mackenzie could be the least bit interested in her? They were polar opposite—he the proverbial representation of all things good and right, while she came from a life in Sin City and had a seriously blurred definition of what constituted as *good*.

She heard the front door open and assumed Wyatt had returned to pick up something more for Aimee's nausea. She'd been happy to help him earlier. Glad he'd trusted her. At least she had that. A swelling of pride bubbled inside her. He was a good man, and so too, Dalton. Which gave her hope that she too, would find her purpose—if not here, then somewhere. With her family's support, she could overcome most anything.

"The ginger should help the nausea," she called out as she padded barefoot to the front door to meet him. To her surprise, Rein emerged from the foyer. She came to an abrupt stop. The minimal light made it difficult to capture his expression. He was the last person she expected to see. "Oh, it's you."

"Wyatt said you were here." He reached up, unfastened his top button and loosened his bolero tie. Unaffected apparently by her icy stare, he sidestepped her and sat down on one of the couches. Releasing a deep sigh, he leaned back and closed his eyes. She had no interest in being alone with him, which of course, was a complete lie. Under different circumstances, she'd have liked nothing better. But things weren't that way between them, and the sooner she accepted that, the less frustrated she'd be. "Wedding too much for you?" She bent down to pick up her shoes that she'd left near where he chose to park himself. Their gazes clashed as she straightened to leave.

"It got a little warm down there. Thought I'd come up and check on the house." He leaned forward, cleared his throat and clasped his hands over his knees.

"Well, I'm leaving anyway. I was just on my way down to see if Betty needs my help." Her shoes dangled in one hand. She turned on her heel to leave and felt his hand on her arm.

"Stay." He looked up at her. "I—uh, wanted to talk to you." His expression slid into a half-embarrassed grimace. "You're not carrying any knives, are you?"

Liberty eyed him. Was he serious? Did he actually believe the crap that Caroline dished out about her? That alone fascinated her, despite the fact that she felt another of his fatherly lectures coming on. She stood her ground, albeit reluctantly. "What have I done wrong now, Dad?"

"I wish you wouldn't call me that."

"Then maybe you should stop treating me like I'm twelve."

He dropped his hold on her arm and brushed his hand through his light brown hair, causing it to stand on end. It was a rare thing to see him without his Stetson. It gave him a less intimidating appearance, until he looked at you, like now, with those piercing blue eyes with green flecks that appeared turbulent when he was riled.

"Look, will you please have a seat. What I have to say won't take up too much of your time."

Stealing herself against more of his criticism, she sat on the couch across from him and propped her feet on the coffee table. Her feet and calves were sore from walking in the god-forsaken heels. Sure, they looked great on stage, but they weren't designed for traipsing around the great outdoors. "Listen, can we just get on with this? Is it the dress, which is your sister-in-law's by the way. Am I wearing my hair wrong? Is my lipstick inappropriate?" Tired both physically and emotionally, she didn't feel like playing nice.

She leaned forward to rub her calves and noted how his eyes dropped to the front of her dress. He coughed and averted his gaze.

"I wanted to apologize."

All the things she'd mentally prepared to sling back at him slid out of her brain. "Pardon? I'm not sure I heard you clearly. Could you hit me with that one more time?" Frustration punctuated his audible sigh. Good. He should feel what it's like. Earlier she might have tossed a shoe at his head, but she wasn't yet ruling out the possibility.

He cleared his throat. "I said I wanted to apologize."

There were so many options available. "For *which time*,

exactly?"

"Betty mentioned you were upset. I think maybe you might have overheard my friend." His gaze held hers. She wasn't about to let him off so easy.

"*You're* the one apologizing for what your friend said?" When he didn't respond right away, she continued. "Or maybe it's because you happen to agree with her?"

"That's not the point."

Liberty threw her shoe at him. He quickly deflected it with his arm. "You're right, it's none of my business. Nothing around here is any of my business. You've made that perfectly clear. Got it." She stood to leave. Enough of this cockamamie bull crap. She needed a drink.

"Sit down."

"Seriously? You're going to pull that on me?"

He stepped over the table and stood toe-to-toe, challenging her. The air between them crackled While visions of falling on the couch in the throes of passion crossed her mind he didn't make a move. Instead, his somber gaze held hers, perhaps in an attempt to intimidate. What he didn't know is that she'd grown up around men who reveled in the art of intimidation. It no longer scared her, and in fact it served as more of a challenge. With Rein, she had a feeling they'd both win. From what she'd come to know about him, he had an underlying passion that drove him as much as what drove her to survive. The melding of the two would be hot, explosive, but not, she surmised, without its destructive properties.

"I just want to talk." The muscle beneath his firm jaw twitched under the strain.

"Pity." She held his gaze a moment longer and sat down. "Happy?" He might act uninterested, but she felt the tension between them. "Aren't you going to sit down?" She realized suddenly that it wasn't her—she'd managed to get along with everyone in the family and most of the townspeople she'd met this week. Yet, Rein remained stubbornly aloof and judgmental around her. Now she wanted to know why.

He braced his hands on his hips and looked at the floor.

"You said you came here to apologize for something?"

"Look I came to apologize for what you might have heard Caroline say."

The corner of her mouth lifted. Suddenly he had a conscience. "Might have? Anyone in a five-foot radius heard her. Lucky for me I got to hear it firsthand. Have a seat, Mackenzie. Let me tell you something you might not realize about me."

The cushions gave as he sat down beside her. His nearness sparked forbidden images of being alone in the dark room, of him easing her back on the couch, his hand sliding beneath the hem of her dress....

She slapped away that thought and inched away from him. "Your friend didn't say anything that I haven't heard before." She offered a short laugh. "I've come to learn that people are critical, maybe even afraid of things, sometimes even people who are different than they are." She eyed him, and his head bent as he listened. "And if I were to guess, I'd say you have the same problem. You just won't admit it."

"Please. I don't have that problem, for your information." He glanced at her and looked away, but not before she saw in his eyes that she'd pegged him.

She sat forward to get his attention. "Right. That's why you've been on my back like some obsessed guidance counselor since I arrived."

He tossed her a disbelieving look. "That's bull."

"And what's more, I suspect that's partly the reason you and Caroline aren't together."

"What the hell does she have to do with this?"

"That's a good question, actually, but not one that I can answer."

"Look, I don't know where you're going with this." He straightened his shoulders and casually dropped his arm over the back of the couch, pretending her words didn't apply to him. Her experience with dancing had taught her to decipher body language. Right now, Rein's screamed defensiveness.

"I guess that makes two of us." She crossed her arms and waited for his response. His gaze met hers and it appeared he had something to say; instead, it came out as a frustrated sigh. Liberty took advantage of his state. She tipped her head, and regarded him. "Why do you feel the need to apologize to me for some idiotic remark made by your *ex*-girlfriend?"

She could almost hear the gears working as he mulled that one over. He stood then, and walked to the old rocking chair that sat near the fireplace. Though late spring Dalton had built a fire earlier in the day, when Aimee stated that the smell calmed her morning sickness. Sadie, the Kinnison's loyal retriever, peered up at him from her doggie bed, her tail thumped soft against the wood floor.

"So, are you avoiding the question, Rein? Or just me?"

"No...maybe. This has been a crazy week. Everyone's been running around all over the place, trying to get things done for the wedding. Meantime, I've been trying to keep the cabin project on schedule, appease Wyatt's concerns about Aimee and the baby." His soft sigh wafted over her heart.

"Not to mention having to prepare for unexpected guests." She referred not only to herself, but to Caroline as well.

He eyed her. "Yeah. That, too."

She waited a moment, debating how best to respond. Maybe she could offer him a little slack. "I guess everyone is tired."

"Yeah." Mundane as was his answer, it served to deflect some of the tension between them. Soft music from the reception drifted through the open door of the deck. He looked at her, his face somber. "She had no right to say those things about you."

Liberty raised a brow, touched he would defend her against the woman's rude comments, yet surprised that he didn't realize how his remark had sounded. "While I appreciate your apparent concern, it wasn't what she said that bothered me nearly as much as your response."

He looked at her, brows pressed together in a frown and shook his head. He didn't remember.

"I believe your exact words were, *"she's a good kid."*

"The truth is, I didn't want to make a scene. It was no more than an offhanded remark to get her to stop talking. I had no idea it would matter to you, anyway."

"You're right. It shouldn't, but it does." Liberty considered the consequences of her next actions. But curiosity about this strange tug and pull between them caused her to stand before him. "Maybe it's because I'm determined to prove to you that I'm not a kid. Can you tell me that you haven't noticed?"

He shot her a brief look, but didn't refute it.

She leaned down and braced her hands on the chair arms, forcing him to look at her. "Or are you too busy trying to find ways *not* to notice?"

"Liberty..." His mesmerizing eyes held hers. "I don't think you know what you're doing."

"You mean if I'm going to climb into the saddle, I better be ready for the ride?" She smiled. "Oh, I'm ready, Rein. You're the one having second thoughts. Are you afraid things are not yet over between you and Caroline?"

A brief laugh escaped him. "Doubtful. I don't think I'm well-traveled enough for her."

"Then Rein, what's your problem?"

He drew in a breath and she could see him battling the attraction simmering between them. It was all she could do to keep from straddling his lap and dominating his sexy mouth. Lord, she wanted to do wicked, sweaty things with him. His gaze dropped lower to the gap in her dress. She wore no bra.

"See something you like?" A simple side zipper was the only barrier between them and utter bliss.

He catapulted from the chair and in an instant had her by the shoulders, lifting her off the floor as he captured her mouth in a fiery kiss. She clamped her arms around his neck, responding to him, meeting his hungry mouth. He grabbed her butt, and a visceral heat slammed into her. She wound her legs around him, sensing his aroused state. His tongue slipped between her lips, turning her bones to ash as their tongues mated in a maddening rush. She gripped fistfuls of his hair, holding his mouth to hers. Then, just as quickly, he released his hold.

"Jesus," he mumbled, drawing in a ragged breath.

She moaned inwardly as she slid down his body. He blinked a few times and took a step back, rubbing his forehead as though berating his actions.

Her skin burned, her emotions still caught up in a lusty whirlwind.

"You ought not to play these games, Liberty. Not with me."

"Is that what you think?" She countered with angry humiliation. "That I'm being a tease?" Hadn't he been the one to kiss her like there was no tomorrow?

"I think you're used to having men focused on you. When one comes along that isn't. I'm not sure you know how to handle it."

"Meaning you, of course? You're telling me that you're not interested."

"Maybe I called your bluff."

She slapped him. Hard. "Now would be a good time for you to leave." Her palm stung, not as bad as his cheek from the way he nursed it. Damn fool, cowboy. Hell, maybe she was the fool. She turned away and swiped an errant tear from her cheek.

He didn't leave. "Listen, Liberty."

She turned her gaze to him. "No. You listen. Stay away. Do you hear? Don't even speak to me." She raised her finger when he opened his mouth. "Don't! I wanted to think that you were different than other men. But you're right. Clearly, as far as you're concerned, I don't belong here. And as soon as I can manage, I intend to put an end to your having to tolerate me."

"Liberty, I said nothing about being here...."

"For the record, I didn't want to come here. If I'd had

76

somewhere else to go, I would've." She gave a caustic laugh. "My mother always spoke so highly of my brothers and about this place. She spoke about Jed as a good man and said that if ever I needed help, that Wyatt and Dalton were good people because Jed had raised them." She wanted to cry, wanted to hit something. But she stood her ground, fists clenched at her sides. He would not see her cry. She wouldn't give him the satisfaction. "Maybe your life was different. Maybe you had a perfect family. But I mine wasn't, not by a long shot. So before you cast judgments on me, because of my age or how I choose to dress or even my profession—start first with the decency of getting to know me as a person."

"I didn't come here to pass judgment."

"Right, you've said all you needed to say. Now, please just go."

She heard his footsteps cross the floor. "And crappy-ass kiss, by the way," she called after him. Total goddamn lie. Her body still tingled, but the anger rolling inside her made it easier to shove the desire away. The front door opened and closed. With her pride and her heart brutally bruised, she collapsed on the couch and buried her face in a pillow to muffle her uncontrolled tears.

೧

She thought he'd come from a perfect family? No question the little scene between him and Liberty made for several nights of restless sleep. He'd granted her wish not to speak to her, which made encounters a bit awkward, particularly in front of family members. But no one asked questions, thankfully, and their eyes met—well, he better understood the term, "If looks could kill."

Rein sat in a camp chair, in the middle of the skeletal cabin structure he'd been working on, staring out at the mountains on the horizon, contemplating the time he'd gone hunting with Jed and came face-to-face with a young grizzly bear. Knocked to the ground, the animal's great paw had slammed across his shoulder blade, leaving behind a searing pain. Fortunately, the heavy coat he'd worn lessened the depth of the slash. As instructed by Jed, he'd covered his head and prayed his uncle would find him before the bear finished him. Somehow, it seemed that maybe this moment had been justified. How could someone come this close to dying—twice? What seemed like an eternity was but seconds when he heard the crack of a rifle and the weight of the bear lifted off him. Later, Michael Greyfeather would call him brave, and tell him because he'd faced his fear, that he and the bear were brothers. After the place on Rein's shoulder healed, Michael took him to have the bear claw inked on his shoulder, reminding him of his courage and its importance to those around him.

That day paled in comparison to facing his mixed up feelings for Liberty.

If he were to be honest, he had as much to be sorry for as Caroline when it came to having prejudices against Liberty. He couldn't put his finger on it exactly. Before, when they were discussing the thought of her coming to stay at the ranch, it seemed like the charitable thing to do. What she'd done for a living, dancing on stage every night for men didn't seem to matter as much—not until after he met her.

Could he be jealous? Could it be that he didn't trust that she could tease men as entertainment and not do the same to him? Dammit. His brain and his body were on different sides of the fence when it came to her. His brain cautioned with reasons and good intent, his body on the other hand, burned for her. Sure, he could take advantage of what she offered. A summer fling. She'd not made any promises about staying, in fact she'd talked about leaving once she got on her feet. Maybe it'd be good for both of them. No strings. No one gets hurt. Problem being, she was Wyatt and Dalton's little sis—and if she did get hurt, there'd be hell to pay.

Rein picked up his uncle's old leather journal weighing it in his hand before he unwound the leather strap holding it shut. He skimmed first over a few of his sketches, read a couple of Jed's notes, effectively avoiding the piece of lined notepaper he knew lay tucked somewhere amid its pages. He hadn't looked at it in years. Hadn't felt the need. But the whole business of the wedding and Liberty's comment about his family, well he knew it wasn't true. His upbringing hadn't been perfect.

A piece of paper slipped from the pages and fell to the floor. His heart squeezed tight knowing the content. The words on the yellowing note were those of a young boy, barely eleven. The psychiatrist had suggested that he get out his recollection of the event on paper, so he could externalize his emotions instead of keeping them inside where they would fester. *Had it been eighteen years?* It seemed like an eternity. It felt like yesterday. Swallowing hard, he carefully unfolded the note and began to read the words of that devastated eleven-year-old boy.

It kind of all started because I wanted to go to summer football camp. My dad thought it'd be good for me. My mom didn't.

"I thought we were past this discussion," my mom said when he brought it up. We were in the car. Dad drove. Mom looked back at me. She was angry. Her lips for—formed—this thin line when she got really mad. She blamed being mad on my "eleven-year-old" behavior. I never understood that.

"Come on, Bev," my Dad said. "It will be good for him. He doesn't have many friends. He needs to get out and socialize." I felt the car as it jarred off the edge of the road. My mom grabbed the dashboard, and glared at my dad.

"Will you pay attention to what you're doing, Liam? These roads are treacherous at night." She leaned forward as though she could help my dad see. "Why on earth did we ever agree to this?"

"Because," Dad said. "We haven't seen your brother Jed in almost five years. The man invited us up for Thanksgiving. We're going."

I tried to reason with her myself. Give Dad a break.

"Mom?" My voice cracked. I remember it doing that when I got upset. I hated it, and I hated my mom for being so lame. "If Uncle Jed agrees I should play, can I?"

She faced forward, her eyes on the road. She didn't answer.

"Will you relax," I heard my Dad say. "There's not a soul out here tonight. Look the road is clear as can be. Now about this football camp, just let the boy play. What harm can there be in that?"

I remember hearing her take a deep breath. It seems so clear to me now. I knew what was coming. The "story". The same excuse she always used. She hated the idea of me playing a sport—any sport. But especially football. It was so unfair.

Rein struggled and stared at the pages, debating whether to continue, but he did, determined that he could disassociate himself from the young boy trying to claw his way back from his guilt.

"You know very well what harm can come of those summer camps. Dehydration, exhaustion, heart problems. You remember what happened to Jonathan, my cousin's boy. Not a thing wrong with him until he started playing high school sports. Then suddenly he's passing out, and then came all the doctor visits, and then they discovered his bad heart."

"Bev, you're being unreasonable. Just because one boy has those problems, doesn't mean Rein will."

My dad understood. But it was no use. She would never give in. I looked out the window and tried to block out the argument that followed. What happened next. I remember in small fragments, like pieces of a puzzle, but some of the pieces are missing. Their voices grew louder in the small car. So loud, I wanted to cover my ears. I wanted to make them stop. God, all I wanted was to be like the other guys in my class. Why couldn't she just let me be like everyone else?

"Just stop," I said. I remember seeing the side of my

mom's face, the way she always wore her blonde hair cut in the same style, just below the ears. Her mouth moved, but I didn't listen. I knew the excuses, the arguments that were once more shooting down my dreams. I hated her at that moment more than anything.

"Shut up!" I screamed it at the top of my lungs. "I hate you! I just wish you would die!" That got their attention. I remember their startled faces looking over the back seat at me, like they were shocked to see me there."

Rein blinked, steeling himself for what came next. He reminded himself, as the psychiatrist and so many others had, that the accident hadn't been his fault. But part of him would always feel responsible.

"They were looking at me. I'm sure they were about to ground me for a month, maybe longer. So, they didn't see it coming. They couldn't see what I saw from the backseat. I couldn't warn them in time. The dump truck. Yellow, I think, maybe orange—came flying out of a dark entrance road. It ran the stop sign I found out later, and barreled straight into the front half of our car.

My head snapped back. I felt like a rag doll thrown across the seat. Then came a loud roar and the sound of shattering glass. I heard the high-pitched screech of metal on metal, like the sound a can makes when it's being crushed, only a thousand times louder. Then, I heard screams. Maybe they were mine. I shut my eyes. I didn't want to know how I was going to die.

Then I waited. I don't remember how long before I opened my eyes. My head felt fuzzy, like I'd been asleep for a long time. But I could still smell the stench of gas and hot rubber.

It was dark, but somewhere above me I saw flashes of light—blue, white, a glimpse of red, and then blue again. Voices. Muffled. Someone called out orders. He sounded mad. In a hurry. Could it have been my Dad? I couldn't tell what was happening.

Somewhere close by, the sound of a chainsaw, its ragged teeth sinking into the metal, shot a fear in me so deep, I thought I'd suffocate from it. My face felt wet. If I'd been crying, I didn't remember. I was scared. So scared. Where were my mom and dad? Were they outside waiting for me?

My chest hurt. Something pressed down on me, making it hard to breathe. I realized one of my hands was free. I fished around looking for something, anything familiar. That's when I found her hand. I knew it was my mom's. I felt her ring and her manicured nails she'd just had done. But in the smoke and rubble, I couldn't see her face. I called out to her.

"Mom." My voice sounded weird. Not like me at all. A hot pain shot through my leg when I tried to move, and I bit my lip to fight screaming out and scaring her any more than she probably was. "Mom, are you okay?" I tried to get a better grip on her hand, relieved when her fingers closed around mine. She was okay. It was going to be okay. But she didn't respond. "Mom! Mom I'm sorry! I'm sorry!" I yelled it over and over. I wanted to cry. It felt like this huge lump was stuck in my throat. I could barely breathe. Tears ran down my face, but I couldn't reach them to wipe them away. I didn't want to let go of her hand.

"I won't go to camp, Mom, I swear. I won't. Just tell me you're okay. Please, Mom. I love you." I began to get scared that I might not make it. That she might not hear what I needed her to hear before I died. The voices grew louder; I tried to hear her tell me that it'd be okay.

"I didn't mean it Mom. I don't hate you. Please, please." I felt the air leave my lungs in a rush. The pressure on my chest lifted and I saw the blood...so much blood.

I still held my mom's hand, but I couldn't see the rest of her body. It was somewhere beneath the massive front tire of the truck. I screamed her name and tasted the blood running down my cheek from a cut on my head. But I gripped her hand tight.

"No. No, you're going to be okay. I love you, Mom." I felt

her fingers squeeze my hand, and then it went limp. I must have blacked out after that, because I woke up in the hospital and my Uncle Jed said that I'd be coming to live with him from now on."

Rein quietly folded the paper and tucked it between the journal's pages. His chest ached. Rubbing his hand over his heart, he looked through the open framework of the window and watched the sunset in the western sky. His eyes stung with fresh tears.

That day changed him. And while Jed had been the best father figure a guy could ever hope for, he wasn't his dad. Despite counseling, and the years that had passed since the accident, Rein still carried a residual guilt. He pressed his fingers against his eyelids and felt nauseous. Old feelings stirred in his gut. How could he have known it would be the last time he'd see them alive?

"Hey man, Wyatt's just about got the steaks done." Dalton walked through the open shell of a front door and looked around. Rein was supposed to be setting the posts for the kitchen wall. "You feeling okay?"

Rein nodded. "Yeah. I'll be good in minute."

Dalton's gaze darted to the journal. There'd been a number of times over the years that Rein had tried to get through the letter without shoving it and his memories aside. Today had been the first time he'd managed to get through to the end. The outcome, like the guilt, remained the same.

Dalton regarded him carefully. "You read it, didn't you?"

Rein went about re-wrapping the strip of leather around the book. He nodded.

"It doesn't get any easier, I know. But Rein, it wasn't your fault, man."

Rein tossed the journal in his workbag, effectively shoving the entire episode the back of his mind. He blew out a deep breath, no longer that scared little boy who'd come to live with his Uncle Jed. "Come on, I'm starving. This might well be one of our last decent meals while those two are off on their honeymoon, unless one of us learns how to cook."

Dalton laughed, seeming to understand his need to let the topic remain where it should—in the past. They walked shoulder to shoulder up the lane to the main house. "With any luck, Liberty can share in the cooking," Dalton remarked "Then again, there's always Betty's café."

Rein figured he'd put his money on take out from Betty's, pretty certain that right now. Liberty would prefer to poison him.

Chapter Six

"*I*'d like to propose a toast." Dalton stood at the end of the massive picnic table Rein had made years ago when he'd first discovered his love for furniture making. Made of cypress, it accommodated up to a dozen people comfortably. Two long benches with short backrests ran the length of the table on either side, with matching single chairs at opposite ends. In its day, Jed had hosted many steak fries for his ranch hands. Not until recently had they resurrected as a gathering spot for family and friends.

"So you think that one wedding toast makes you a pro at this now?" Wyatt joked as he dropped his arm over the backrest behind Aimee.

A smile lifted the corner of Dalton's mouth. "A toast to Aimee," he said, raising his beer bottle. "To the woman who has brought new happiness to our family, first by rescuing my sorry-ass brother...."

Wyatt quietly lifted his hand behind his wife and flipped Dalton off.

"And by giving us more happiness to look forward to."

Wyatt raised his glass of lemon water, joining his wife in abstaining from beer.

"Why Dalton Kinnison, I believe that's the sweetest thing I've ever heard you say." Aimee reached out her glass to touch his bottle.

"And good God in heaven, I hope that changing diapers is going to be a helluva whole lot easier than listening to you getting sick every morning."

Aimee chuckled and leaned her head against Wyatt's shoulder.

Dalton's gaze moved around the table. "It used to be just the three of us, but seems like each day our family is expanding. I like to think that Jed would be happy with the way things are turning out." Rein noted that his brother's eyes landed on Liberty. "To family." A reverent response of raised glasses followed from Dalton, Michael and Rebecca Greyfeather, Liberty, Wyatt and Aimee. Rein joined in reluctantly avoiding Liberty's gaze.

"This brings up an idea that I wanted to run past you all, especially you Liberty and of course, Rein." He leaned around his wife to speak directly to his newly discovered half-sister. "I know you haven't been here long and that you may not have made up your mind about what it is you want to do. But I hoped maybe that I could convince you—we could convince you—to stay on at least through the summer. We thought maybe you could put some of those design skills of yours to work by helping Rein with the interiors of the cabins."

"And I'd love having the help with the baby coming," Aimee chimed in with a smile.

Rein's fork stopped short of his mouth. *What the hell?*

"Hey, that's not a bad idea." Dalton piped in. "Save me from buttin' heads all the time with Rein the Impossible. I like the idea. What do you say?"

Rein stuffed a chunk of steak in his mouth, pretending to take his time eating it, until it all but dissolved in his mouth. He realized then how the conversation had stopped and all eyes were on him. He swallowed and chugged a swig of his beer.

"Well, guess we've heard from everyone but you," Wyatt stated. "What do you think? Could you use a little help?"

Clearing his throat, he avoided looking at Liberty. "To be honest, I'm not sure we have the same vision of how these cabins should look. My style is more local tradition, while hers is likely to be more...well, modern."

He caught Wyatt's curious look before he passed a side-look to his wife.

"Thank you, Wyatt, I appreciate the offer," Liberty interjected into the awkward silence. "That's a lovely offer, and I would have considered it, had Betty not already asked me to help her with renovations on the café. She's also offered me a part-time waitressing position. However, if your offer to stay in one of the cabins still stands, I would really appreciate being able to live here. And of course, I'd be happy to pay rent."

He stopped her with his hand and glanced at Rein. "You're welcome to stay as long as you need. That was our arrangement. And congratulations, I'm glad Betty saw fit to give you a chance with your designs."

Maybe reading the letter, dredging up the past made left him feeling disconnected, singled out. What irked the hell out of him was that he was Jed's own nephew and Wyatt hadn't even bothered to speak with him first about his idea. "If you'll excuse me, I've got chores to do." He picked up his plate and after a brief stop in the kitchen to drain his beer, trudged down to the barn.

Wyatt found him there a few moments later. Rein felt his presence, but continued to groom his horse. Whatever the reason —Liberty, the letter, getting behind on his self-imposed deadline, something had set him on edge. And when it came to Liberty, lines became blurred and frustration generally followed. And, right now, discussing that frustration with her older brother was the last thing Rein wanted to do.

"What is your problem with Liberty?"

The horse whinnied in protest when he brought the brush down a little too hard on the mare's side.

"Not a thing." He offered a quick glance at Wyatt.

"You're ticked because I didn't talk to you first about asking Liberty to stay on."

He shrugged. "Might've been nice."

"Didn't think it'd disagree with you, being how you were her greatest ally when we were discussing whether to invite her here in the first place. You do remember that?"

"I do." He moved to the mane, using short strokes to work out the knots in the silky, dark brown hair.

"Something change that I should know about?"

Rein wondered if Liberty had spilled the news of their kiss to Aimee. "Not really. Just prefer to work alone on the design end of things. You know me. I have the ideas in my head until they begin to emerge on my workbench." How could he tell him that Liberty wasn't the problem, but how he reacted around her that concerned him? He didn't trust himself. "Besides, she hasn't really got a lot of experience." Hell, maybe she had a ton of experience for all he knew, but for lack of a better excuse, he tossed it out there.

Wyatt settled himself on the wood trunk where they kept the grooming supplies. "Well for the sake of argument, there are some who would argue that to gain experience, you need to start somewhere."

"Well, I don't have time to take her under my wing and teach her. It would throw my schedule completely off, and this project would take twice as long to finish with her underfoot."

"Underfoot, huh?"

He felt Wyatt's gaze on him. "Yeah, you know what I mean."

Wyatt placed a piece of fresh straw between his teeth. "This doesn't have anything to do with the incident the night of the wedding, does it? Because I've got to tell you, Rein. I'm a little concerned if there's something you think I should be aware of. Is there something Liberty's said or done that's caused you to feel apprehensive about her? Do I need to speak with her? I'm getting ready to whisk my wife away on a much deserved honeymoon and I'd like to know you can handle things around here."

Rein's mind darted back to the night and that kiss. His body tightened at the memory of her mouth on his, the taste of her lips, how she'd clung to him. And had taunted him. Such news would likely create a ruckus that none of them needed right now, not with Wyatt and Aimee preparing to go on their honeymoon. Besides, it wasn't anything that he couldn't handle as long as he kept his wits about him.

"Listen, everything's going to be fine. You guys go on your honeymoon and don't worry about things here."

Wyatt nodded. "I have no doubt that you guys can handle the ranch. I guess maybe seeing how much Liberty's helped Aimee these past few days and all her help with the wedding and the reception, I think Jed would have welcomed her just like he did us."

Rein waved his brother off the trunk and tossed the brush in. "Suspect you're right about that."

"Aimee indicated Liberty's old boyfriend—her boss—I understand, is a real piece of work. Course, I don't expect it's ever a good idea to get involved with your boss, but she's young and she'll learn. She ever talk to you about her past, or her father?"

Rein shrugged. "Not really. Just that they didn't get along. Guess there's a lot we don't know about her. Maybe I've been thinking more about that due to Aimee's condition, you know?" Rein took a deep breath and finally met Wyatt's eyes. He'd been pouring out one excuse after another, trying to convince himself that he had no interest in their little sister. And the comment about not messing around with the boss? Yeah, that didn't settle too well inside him, either.

"You let me worry about Aimee and the baby. Maybe you can get Liberty to open up to you." He slapped him on the shoulder. "You're going to have your hands full between her and Dalton. They're two of a kind in some ways."

Rein followed his brothers departing form. Yet another thing to add to his list of reasons why he shouldn't get involved with Liberty.

CR

"Miss? Miss? Could I get a refill on my water?" She glanced up and caught Dalton's ornery grin. She ripped off the customers receipt and left it at the table.

"Tell Betty we love the new look," the woman remarked.

"I will thank you." Liberty sauntered over to Dalton, grabbing a water pitcher from one of the old cupboard stations set up around the room. Tempted to pour it over his head, she picked up his glass and eyed him. "You figure out what you're going to order yet? You can't just sit here and razz me without ordering."

"Never bothered, Betty." Dalton gave her a wink.

"Who cooks your food?" She raised her brow and glanced outside. "Rein working again?"

Dalton studied the menu. "Yeah, he stayed up working all night in cabin three again, trying to get the kitchen cabinets installed. This new menu is great, but I don't recognize the names anymore."

"It's part of Betty's plan to spruce things up and bring in tourists." Liberty's mind was elsewhere, envisioning Rein, in his t-shirt and jeans and that damn baseball cap he wore when he worked, sweating over his sander.

"Which, by the way, looks fantastic," Dalton replied. "I like what you've done with the place. The antique sideboards and those antler chandeliers really give it a rustic elegant look. Rein would be impressed."

She glanced at him offering a short laugh. "Yeah, I bet he would."

"Listen, is this Montana Burger any good?"

"We are talking Betty here, you understand."

"Make it two, and hang on to the fries. Need to save room for dessert. Rebecca bring in any fresh pie today?"

Liberty nodded, wondering if she could impress Rein with

anything she did. So far, nothing had worked. "I'll check to see what's left."

She took his menu and started to leave.

"Don't let him get to you, Liberty."

"Who?" she lied.

Dalton tipped his head, pinning her with a look that said he knew better. "Rein. He can be a stubborn old coot. He's dealing with wanting to get things in before winter, and I think maybe his pride might be a little bruised that Wyatt didn't discuss the idea of you working together before he brought it up in front of everyone."

She shrugged. "I understand. You think in time, he'll come around then?"

Dalton nodded. "Sure. Hey, I know. Why don't we all head over to Dusty's on Friday night. We could play some pool and have a couple of beers. I want to introduce my little sis around."

Liberty's heart warmed with belonging. She bit the corner of her lip to keep from letting her eyes well. "We'll see how things are around here, ok? Betty might need me to work late."

"Sure." He grinned, and then added. "If you got it, Rein's favorite is pecan pie."

Did Dalton see something more that she hadn't been able to regarding Rein? She didn't feel comfortable yet opening up about her feelings regarding Rein. Besides, if she left, was there anything really to discuss? But Aimee's plea for her to stay until the baby was born, to help Betty, and the kindness of the folks in this small town had gotten under her skin. The only thing still causing a burr in her side— Rein Mackenzie.

❧

She'd forgotten how much she loved the music. Liberty sat in a booth opposite of Dalton, nursing her bottle of beer, her attention diverted from watching the front door each time a young woman stopped by to say hello to her handsome half-brother. "Do you know every woman in this state?" She regarded Dalton's dark eyes, the same as Wyatt's and hers, she noted. His grin displayed a cocky pride.

"Montana's a big state. I've barely started."

She chuckled at his attitude. Clearly, from the number of folks who'd stopped by the table—male and female—that the Kinnison's were well known and liked, it appeared.

"Hey, sorry about the game. Had no idea they had a tournament going on." His smile widened. "You don't want to get in on that action, by chance?"

She held her hand up, halting the idea. "No, no. I haven't played in a quite a while. I'm a little rusty. But I'll challenge you one of these days. Maybe after I've had some time to practice."

"Yeah." He picked up his beer and looked around. "If you think it will help you."

One of the girls Liberty worked with at Betty's appeared at the booth with a tray of fried dill pickles that Dalton had ordered.

"I didn't know you worked here," Liberty acknowledged the young woman.

"I'm filling in as a favor. The tournament brought in more people than they expected tonight. Dusty called over to Betty's to see if she could spare some help. It's a little extra income for me. Will there be anything else?" She addressed Dalton with a smile.

"Keep the tab running," he said and dropped a five on her tray. He lifted his hand and waved at a beautiful dark haired woman across the room. "Liberty, would you excuse me a moment. There's someone I haven't seen since last Christmas."

She waved him away and smiled as her co-worker cleared away empty bottles from the table next to them. "You suppose he could use more help? I'm pretty good behind a bar."

"I don't know, I can ask. He sure looks as though he could use the help."

She drained her beer and nodded. "Let's go see." If nothing else, it would keep her mind off other matters—namely her obsession with whether Rein Mackenzie would possibly come walking through that door. The crowd at the bar was at least three people deep. They had to push their way through the mass to find a spot where they could squeeze behind the bar.

"Hey Dusty, this is Liberty Kinnison." The girl stated.

Liberty started to correct her, but felt it pointless given the din of the bar.

"You can call me Liberty." She leaned forward and shouted. "Looks like maybe you could use a hand."

"You know your way around a bar?"

She nodded. "Trained with some of the best out in Vegas."

He tossed her a towel. "You're hired."

That, as they say—was that. The waitress ducked back in the kitchen. Liberty faced a thirsty crowd.

"You know how to make a Hurricane?" Dusty asked.

"Coming up." She began choosing the bottles and in short time, had memorized most of them and found her rhythm, taking orders with ease. She enjoyed the lively bar. The patrons were friendly, the jukebox blasted out a blend of classic and country rock and she found herself laughing as she danced around the cook and cut up with Dusty behind the bar.

She glanced up to find Dalton back at the booth, joined now by Sally. She thought of Rein working alone at the ranch, bent over the sawhorse, the sweat on his muscular arms glistening as he pushed the blade through the wood. He probably wore one of his standard issue grey t-shirts, which he must have a million of, and had that idiotic tool belt wrapped around his lean hips. She closed her eyes and leaned a hand on the counter.

"You okay?" Dusty asked. She took a deep breath and with a nod, struggled to reel in her thoughts. That kiss, the way Rein had looked at her that night like he wanted to consume her was seared into her memory and she feared, into her heart as well. She'd tried to convince herself that it didn't matter—

he didn't matter. Hell, he didn't even think she should stay, or at least he hadn't tried to get her to change her mind when she mentioned leaving. It seemed that only Wyatt and Aimee, even cynical Dalton that wanted her to stay.

She chuckled to herself. Maybe Rein was right, maybe she did want what she couldn't have. She blew out a sigh, redirecting her thoughts and decided to give the folks at End of the Line a little taste of what she'd learned in Vegas.

She pulled out all the stops and began to show off her skills—tossing bottles behind her back, performing feats of balance and jaw-dropping stunts as she concocted drink requests from the delighted crowd. She enjoyed the fast pace, and would have pursued the profession had Angelo not insisted that she made more money on the stage than behind the bar. But what she'd learned under the wing of the bartenders at the club was the social skills required to be a top-notch bartender. As such, it didn't take her long to learn the names of the locals and what they preferred to drink.

Numbers around the bar had increased, pressing in with applause and smartphone flashes taking her picture. Between the chants and the wicked music, Liberty realized the people wanted a show. She glanced at Dusty who stood grinning from ear-to-ear as he watched from the other end of the bar. She had the place in the palm of her hand. With a toss of a bottle, she spun on her heel, catching it in time to the music, holding it precariously high above the martini shaker. More whistles and a slow chant of "go Liberty" erupted, fueling her confidence. One last ingredient left. With a grin, she grabbed the bottle and slung it in a sweeping arch over her head. The move, though tricky, she'd practiced over and over until she'd perfected it to her standards. The idea being that she'd bump the bottle upward with her shoulder and catch it in her other hand.

The bar community in a singular voice rose in a deafening chorus of "ah" as she looked up seeing the bottle sailing high overhead. She glanced over the sea of bodies and saw Dalton seated at the end of the booth, his wide grin showing his pride. Sally sat across from him, her eyes wide, hands wrapped around her drink. Then her gaze slammed into Rein's stormy blue eyes. He wore no expression as he watched. She might as well have been invisible. She missed the catch and to the unified disappointment of the patrons, the bottle crashed to the floor. Humiliated, she stared at the mess and finally shook her head.

Dusty nudged her arm with a broom. "Better luck next time. You're pretty damn good, kiddo."

"Yeah." Embarrassed, but more frustrated than anything that one look from Rein Mackenzie could discombobulate her, she set to cleaning up the glass.

"Hey, hot shot." Dalton leaned over the counter and looked down at her. "When you're finished, come on back to the table. I'll buy you a beer."

She wasn't about to give Rein the opportunity to further dig into her, especially in front of his ex. Liberty swept up the shards, trying her best to stay out of Dusty's way. She felt suddenly conspicuous, as though she had "outsider" emblazoned on her forehead. No one had said anything to make her feel as much, it'd been engrained in her.

Making her feel like an outcast had been her father's favorite head game. After her mother died, he told her she'd been an accident, her mother's greatest disappointment and he eventually blamed her for her mother's suicide.

Liberty had found her after returning home from a night out with friends. Dropping her bag on the pristine white couch, she noticed the unusual quiet, but surmised her mom might be at her spin class or out shopping. She grabbed a glass of ice water and sauntered past the master bedroom, peeking in just in case her mother should still be sleeping.

Stunned by what she saw, she didn't feel the glass slip from her hands, until it shattered on the stone tile floor. Her mother lay in her nightgown, sprawled across the bed. A vodka bottle and her sleeping pills container empty beside her.

She'd left no note, no good-byes, and no apologies. But Liberty knew why. The mistakes of her mother's past—one that included leaving Jed and her boys—and the torture of her abusive husband that had driven her to this extreme. She'd been forbidden to speak of her sons. It wasn't permitted. But in private, her mother had shown her a box that she'd kept hidden.

The night Liberty left, she tucked those mementos, including a letter addressed to her sons, in her duffle bag. It had the ranch's address, but hadn't been sent. Liberty read it on the bus. Their mother had written to tell them they had a half-sister and the choice of her words made her wonder if her mother still loved Jed. Whether true or not, it was evident that she still cared and appreciated him for adopting her sons. She knew he'd take care of them better than she'd been able to give them most of their lives.

Liberty hadn't shown the letter to Wyatt and Dalton yet. She'd been waiting for the best time. Despite Eloise's regrets and her confession to Liberty that she'd made some poor choices, didn't mean that her sons would automatically accept and trust Eloise's daughter. She finished cleaning up and apologized again to Dusty. "I'm really sorry about the mess. I'd like to pay to replace the liquor." Dusty dismissed her concerns with a wave of his hand.

"Hey, it can happen on a slow night. You're always welcome here. Might be fun to have you doing your thing during the holidays." Dusty said. "That's when we really pull in a load of people, with families visiting and what not.

"Aimee started up an annual New Year's Eve fundraiser to restock the food pantry. We hope she'll be able to spearhead another one this year, but we'll have to see with the baby and all. Anyway," he continued, wiping down the bar, "come on by, if you're still around. Might be fun and it's for a good cause."

"Thanks, Dusty. I'll think about it." She walked up to the table, aware that Rein and Sally were engaged in something of a private joke. She tapped Dalton on the shoulder. "Hey, I'm beat, would you mind taking me home?"

Dalton took one look at her and nodded. "Sure, let's go."

"I'll drive." She held out her hand for the keys. With a frown, he relinquished them.

"Are you sure you won't stay for one drink?" Sally asked.

Rein studied the bottle he twirled slowly between his hands. He didn't look at, much less speak, to her.

"Another time, maybe, thanks. Night, Rein." She forced out a civil goodbye.

He glanced up with a quick nod, and then looked at his brother. "I'll be home soon."

Chapter Seven

"*B*oy, you could have cut the tension between the two of you with a butter knife. What's going on?" Sally shifted in her seat and gave Rein her don't-give-me-any-crap-teacher look.

He took a pull of his beer, and eyed her. "You probably hadn't heard yet, but Miss Liberty has requested that I steer clear of her."

Shock registered on her face. "What on earth...why?" Her gaze narrowed. "Rein Mackenzie, what did you say to her?"

He thought before he responded. He didn't need another female lambasting him just now and if he told Sally the truth, she'd be all over him. As if he hadn't already been battling the guilt of what he'd said to Liberty and how poorly he'd handled things between them. But that unexpected, explosive kiss scared the daylights out of him, and its intensity caused him to react in an attempt to protect her—to keep her as far from him as possible.

Hell, given another minute, he'd have likely taken her right there on the floor. Awkward as things now were, it had worked, except for the tormented dreams he'd been having all week. He tried to justify his pent-up frustration by searching for other things to find distasteful about her. Anything that might help put his lust in better perspective. "You ever notice she hasn't opened up a bank account? That she pays cash for everything. She's never asked for a dime from any of us, that I know of. Don't you find it a little peculiar?"

"She's working," Sally remarked dryly. "And had probably saved up something from her work in Vegas."

His mind raced trying to figure out how much a dancer of Liberty's persuasion would make at a successful nightclub. No doubt, she'd garner plenty of tips with that body. His imagination leapt to her in a G-string, strutting across a stage in four-inch heels, those long legs encased in thigh high stockings. In the process, oblivious to present reality, he missed his mouth, sending a steady stream of beer down the front of his shirt. "Dammit, now see what you made me do?"

"Me? I didn't...." She stared at him as though he'd lost his mind.

Truth be told, he was pretty damn close.

Sally rested her arm over the back of the booth. "You know what this sounds like to me?"

"No, and I don't want to know."

"Too bad, because I'm going to say it anyway."

His soaked shirt clung to his chest. "Make your point, since you seem to think you have me all figured out."

"You forget who you're speaking to, Rein."

He met her steady gaze. "I'm sorry. I've got a lot on my mind these days."

"As if that isn't clear." She pointed to his shirt. "Look I'm no expert on these things, but it sounds like maybe you are looking for every possible thing to find wrong with that girl. Don't you think she's figured that out? She's just trying to find her way, Rein. Surely, you can remember what that's like."

He did, and that wasn't the entire issue, but he was hesitant to open up to Sally. He had to deal with the battle going on inside him about what his role should be around her. Could he continue to pretend to be her boss, her mentor as Wyatt asked him to be? Or would he have to face the fact that not since Caroline, had he wanted a woman this bad.

"I gotta go. See you around."

Gripping the wheel, Rein had a hard time focusing on driving and not letting his mind wander to the sexy image of Liberty featured in a single spotlight, her body—toned and tanned—captivating everyone in the audience.

Everyone, but him.

He slammed on the brakes just in time preventing from smashing into the back of Dalton's truck parked outside the main house. He hopped out, grabbed his flashlight and headed toward the unfinished cabin he'd been working on when Sally called and asked him to come up to Dusty's.

"Dalton went inside to make himself a sandwich. I'm sure he'd make you one if you're hungry."

Startled by the feminine voice he pointed his flashlight toward the sound and found Liberty coming down the front porch steps. She shielded her eyes from the bright light. "He'd planned on walking me to my cabin, but if you're headed that way, would you mind if I walked with you?"

He tugged at his shirt, partially dry now, but still reeking of beer. "Sure." They walked down the inky black lane. Rein watched the light bounce off the dirt road with each step. He cleared his throat. The silence was aggravating, but he didn't know how to make things right. Had they ever been? Would they ever be? Could they ever be? Not from his point of view they couldn't. "You seem to know your way around bartending." He tried to keep the conversation light. They weren't that far from her cabin.

"I took a six week course offered once at one of my dad's hotels. It's one of those skills I figure I could fall back on if I need it."

"Is that how you ended up at the strip club...er...the nightclub? Is that what you call it?"

She halted and he didn't need a light to know she glared at him.

"So we're back to what I used to do for a living?"

Rein tipped up his Stetson. "What do you mean?"

"I mean, you seem to have an infatuation with my previous

work as a dancer." She took a step closer, her face illuminated by the circle of light. She tipped her head, curiosity sparkling in those dark eyes. "Or maybe you're just curious to see for yourself."

He snorted a response, swung the light to the path and began to walk. "Hardly darlin'. I prefer my women just a bit older."

"Seriously? Did you just pull that card again?" He felt a slap on the back of his head. His good hat flew off, tumbling to the ground. "At least I haven't sequestered myself in these mountains with nothing but myself and cows to talk to."

"Steers, mostly. Beef cattle. Cows are for milk, generally speaking."

"You...I don't care!" She tossed her arms in the air. "Whatever the hell they're called. I'm really getting tired of your judgmental bullshit. You do know what bullshit is, right?"

He picked up his hat and tapped against his leg. She did have the Kinnison temper.

"What is it exactly that you don't like about me, *Mr. Mackenzie?*"

"This is not a conversation I want to have right now, and my name is Rein."

"Yeah? I'm just trying to show my respect to my elders." She shot past him, full steam ahead toward her cabin.

"I never said I didn't like you," he called after her. That was the truth. He just came unglued in her presence. Hell, he'd come undone a time or two alone at night when she popped into his thoughts.

"Yeah? You have a damn funny way of making a girl feel welcome."

He sighed. He'd maybe had one too many beers, but that wasn't causing him to push her buttons. Better off for her to be mad at him, if he couldn't have her. And he'd convinced himself—nearly—that it would be wrong on so many levels to want her.

She stopped suddenly and whirled on her heel to face him. He had to raise his arms to prevent from stabbing her with the flashlight. Instead, he stood there in surrender to her body brushing against his, and not in a tender way. She looked ready to knock heads, his in particular. She stood close enough that he could tell she'd worn no bra under her layered cami's and tee shirt.

"What do you want from me, anyway?"

Rein swallowed. His lust ticked off at least top five choices before his brain stepped in to remind him that she was off limits. "Nothing." He licked his lips. Damn, if he couldn't use a beer, maybe a shot of something stronger. "I don't want a thing from you."

"For what it's worth, I am of legal age—beyond in fact, and old enough to make my own choices." She pushed her face closer, challenging him in more ways than one. "You know, I think maybe it's *you* that's confused. I think it's *you* that doesn't know what he wants."

"You're taking what I said the wrong way." Damn, that sounded lame even to him. She nudged him chest-to-chest, and held his gaze. He didn't dare lower his arms for fear he'd grab her and never let her go. Jesus, he was going insane.

"Am I?" She waited a moment, torturing him with the mind-sucking scent of her perfumed skin. He tried to be cool, laugh off her driving him mad with her closeness, but the resulting grimace came because of the painful tightening below his belt.

"What are you doing, Liberty? More games?"

She slid her hand over his chest, toying with his collar. Her fingernails gently scraped the place where his pulse beat wild against his neck. "I'm not sure you're man enough for me, darlin'." She let the last word slide off her tongue slow and deliberately. The sweet scent of peppermint clung to her breath. Offering a quick and dirty laugh, she snatched the flashlight from him, turned around and stomped off alone to her cabin, plunging him and his frustrated libido in the dark.

A moment later, the lights went on inside and he saw her silhouette outlined as she stepped out of the front door. "Good night, Mr. Mackenzie. Try not to fall in any holes."

The beam from the flashlight spun through the air and the heavy metal casing nearly beamed him. He grappled with trying to catch it so it wouldn't fall to the ground, unaware he had company.

"*Mr. Mackenzie?*" Dalton walked up behind him, another flashlight in his hand. "Damn, boy. Did you go and piss her off again?"

"Yeah, well she gets pissed easily."

Dalton's chuckle rumbled low in the dark. "God knows you're never antagonistic."

Rein tugged off his hat and raked a hand through his hair. "Yeah, she's different. Stubborn, and with an attitude a mile wide." He glanced at Dalton. "Not like anyone else I know."

Dalton laughed quietly. "Maybe so. But I think she's okay."

"I don't have any issues with your sister, Dal. I just can't let her push my buttons." He started down the lane.

"Absolutely bro, unless you happen to like it."

Rein stopped and looked over his shoulder, the flashlight illuminated Dalton's wide smile. "For the record, I don't."

His brother shrugged. "Just sayin.' Seems like you two spend an awful lot of time sparrin' with each other."

"You've had too many beers." Rein waved away the comment. He didn't want to think any more about this tonight. He wanted to lose himself in his work. Do something constructive. Blow off some steam.

"I only had two and I've got eyes, Rein. Not sure what you think, but I can tell when a woman is interested in a guy."

He refused to entertain the thought. Not tonight. "I'm going down to cabin three and do some work."

"Hey, Rein, for the record. You should stop up to Betty's and see what she's done with the place. New uniforms, new menu, looks pretty good. Liberty has quite a talent."

"I'm sure she did a fine job."

"You know, you can be as hard-headed as her."

"Kiss my ass, Dalton. See you in the morning."

"Sweet dreams, bro. I'll be up here in civilization, if you need me."

In no mood to tolerate Dalton's teasing, Rein trudged past her cabin, jerking his gaze away when he saw her pass by the window. She might well be talented in many ways, but the woman screamed trouble. She was a free spirit, and did not intend to stick around. Theoretically, that should please him, but it only frustrated him more. Dammit.

He'd never been a loner like Wyatt. He enjoyed all kinds of people, had friends. Maybe seeing Caroline again, made him think twice about making that kind of commitment, giving himself to someone. Hell, maybe that was the *one* thing he and Liberty had in common. He had goals, his uncle's dream to finish. She wanted to start a new life. Neither of them appeared to want any strings.

And *that* scared the hell out of him.

He snapped on the overhead light and in short order had changed into his grungy jeans and a worn comfortable tee shirt—standard issue when he did his woodworking. He plastered his ball cap on his head backwards and made a beeline for the sanding project he'd left earlier when curiosity got the better of him, and he went up to Dusty's Place. It would've been wiser if he'd stayed home. He'd not been able to take his eyes off Liberty behind the bar, laughing and cutting up as she juggled bottles with ease, until of course, she stumbled on his gaze and he'd thrown her off her game. He'd felt like some kind of pervert, thinking about her, that kiss and where it might have led had he not stopped it.

When she caught him staring and dropped the bottle, he didn't know whether to feel more guilt or be pleased that he had some kind of effect on her. He hadn't tried to stir up these feelings. With just a look she could turn him inside out. Denying this attraction gnawed a hole in his gut and he didn't know how to deal with it.

With that one kiss, he'd opened up a Pandora's Box, and being ordered to stay away from another taste was akin to waving a red flag in his face. He opened the sliding door and looked out on the small patch of land that would eventually have a flagstone patio. A cool breeze washed over him, and for a moment, he closed his eyes absorbing the wet, mossy scent of the dark forest. This was his serenity, his calm and it had been since the day his uncle took him in. Jed taught all three of his sons to have pride and understand the value of taking ownership in what you've worked hard to build.

With that in mind, Rein set to work, enjoying the fluid heat that burned his muscles as he used the electric sander to smooth a set of bookshelves he'd built to frame the fireplace. Seeing each cabin come to life from his sketches, brought back memories of listening to Jed and his dreams of the Last Hope Ranch. He wanted to carry that through in his designs, making sure to implement the beauty of nature and Montana's rich traditions and history. He utilized timber from dead-standing lodge pole pine and recycled barn board to create his furnishings, using traditional wood builder's techniques of mortise and tenon joining as well as dovetail joints. Recycling and antiques also became one of his passions—using the past to serve in new and innovative ways. Only cabins one and two were livable at this point. With Tyler working on electricity and plumbing in this cabin, Rein hoped to have an additional fourth cabin framed in before winter. With each cabin came the added task of lengthening the narrow road connecting each cabin to the main house, making it accessible in all seasons.

He flipped off the sander and straightened, wincing as he did and rubbed his hand across his lower back. He'd been bent over for—he glanced at his cell phone—over an hour. Heaving a weary sigh, he scanned the room, seeing in his mind's eye what he hoped to accomplish. His gaze landed on a brown portfolio laying on the kitchen cabinet.

Wiping the hem of his tee shirt over his face, he pulled a

bottle of water from the fridge and focused on the folder. He didn't recognize it, but maybe Tyler had left it. Curious, he opened it and studied the soft colored-pencil renderings of the cabin's interior. Extraordinarily professional, with exquisite detail, he realized that they were by Liberty's hand.

Had she left it there on purpose to prove a point? He studied the drawings, impressed that the artist had captured a perfect blend of contemporary with the old west in color and texture choices. The fact that the artist was Liberty gave him pause to consider that he'd been too quick to judge her inexperience, her ability to understand his concept for this project.

Which posed yet another challenge. How could he work closely with her on the cabins and keep from wanting to touch her? Up until now, he'd given himself every excuse under the sun why he shouldn't, but he couldn't deny the power behind that kiss. Since, the tension between them had been akin to getting close to an electric fence. It looks innocent enough when you're looking at it, but one touch could be lethal. He thought he heard music and walked over to the open screen. Staring out into the darkness his eyes traveled up to the dark sky littered with stars. The beauty of this place never ceased to amaze him. That's what his uncle had wanted to share with the world.

His saw first the light pouring out over the landscaped lawn of Liberty's cabin. The music originated from the open patio door. He chewed the corner of his lip, debating the wisdom of where his thoughts were taking him. If he could set aside his pride, he could really use her help.

By leaving her to work on the interiors, shop and order what they needed, she would free up his time for the construction end of things. By virtue of these sketches, she was good, damn good, and it wouldn't kill him to play nice and tell her so. Maybe it could also help ease some of the tension. Then again, it might make things a whole hell of a lot worse.

He tapped the doorframe with his the heel of his hand. It

was clear what he needed to do. Polishing off the water, he unfastened his tool belt, grabbed the folder, and headed out the back door.

With enough light between the two cabins, he walked down a small incline and sidestepped the group of chairs surrounding a cozy fire pit. The slow sultry beat beckoned to him, reverberating in his chest as he got close to the back door. The seductive beat curled around his senses, playing havoc with his imagination.

He reminded himself that he'd come for a reason—a specific reason. He stopped, glancing at the file in his hand and remembered—a quick apology, an offer to work on the décor and he'd be on his way. Stepping up to the door, he looked through the screen and his heart faltered, while other parts leapt into overdrive. Barefoot, in denim cutoffs and a cami that left nothing to the imagination Liberty danced, blissfully unaware she had an audience. His mouth went bone dry, the thrum of his heart sucked into the backbeat. Lord, she was insanely beautiful.

Her phone buzzed, startling both her and him. He felt like a kid caught with his hand in the cookie jar. As she started to answer it, her eyes lifted to his. A tiny gasp, indicating her surprise escaped her mouth, though it was short-lived. Not accepting the call, she placed it on the table, her gaze narrowing on his.

"You been standing there long?" She eyed him, one hand on her hip as she lowered the volume of the music..

Rein had to think for a moment where, who, and why, he was there. "Long enough." He wiped his mouth, fearing he'd been drooling, blinked and held up the folder. "I found this in the cabin. I thought we should talk. Mind if I come in?"

She tipped her head. "Sure." She watched him a moment more then went back to shuffling through her cd collection. He walked in, feeling like a stranger in the very place he'd designed and built.

CB

"You like to dance?" She kept her eyes on her CDs, in a futile attempt to ease the pounding of her heart. The look in his eyes had been predatory, the set of his jaw firm on his stoic face. She felt the tension radiating off him from where she stood. *Long enough?* She wanted to ask him to explain his comment. Dancing on stage had been her profession, but offstage—a type of release, how she rid herself of pent-up frustration. And this guy was the very reason she'd been tied up in knots for weeks, and not the kind they both might enjoy.

"Not especially." He slid open the screen door, stopping to test that it fit the frame, properly. Such a stickler for perfection. She both admired and detested that attribute of his. It was evident in how he designed and constructed his work and on a personal level, she just bet his standards were as meticulous. How he'd reacted after that kiss made it clear to her that she'd never be able to meet those standards.

He gave her a cursory glance. "Do you have a beer?"

She nodded toward the fridge. "Help yourself." A thin line darkened the center back of his grey tee shirt. Her mouth lifted at the image of him bent over his sawhorse, working diligently on another project. The fabric hugged his muscles, moving with them as he leaned down to retrieve a drink. She followed the line of sweat with an appreciative gaze to where it met the top of his waistband. It'd been bad enough to have tossed and turned with the memory of how delicious he'd looked in that tux, but the fit of those worn jeans and that old tee shirt made her fingers itch, imagining his firm body beneath. "You seemed to like dancing with Caroline." Her mumbled comment popped out without a thought and she hoped he hadn't heard it. He had.

He turned, pinning her with that tempest blue-green gaze. "*That* is none of your business."

Her pride challenged, or so it seemed whenever they were in a room together more than five minutes, stiffened her back.

She held up her hand to deflect his comment. "I wouldn't dream of interfering."

"Good." He took a long drink and wiped his mouth with the back of his hand. "There's nothing there to interfere with.

Boy, she wanted to ask more about that, but she dared not. No stranger to sexual tension, she'd learned through her profession how to draw in a man's attention simply by reading his face by making a connection. Rein was a different story. Trying to read him was like driving a dark, winding road at eighty miles an hour, at the mercy of what lay around the next curve.

"It's late. What'd you need to talk about that couldn't wait 'til morning?" She glanced at the clock seeing it well past midnight.

He eyed her as he took a long pull from his beer. "These." He dropped the folder on the cabinet. "I assume you left them in the cabin for me to see?"

She glanced at the folder, recognizing it. "That's mine, yes. Just a few ideas I've tinkered with. But I didn't leave them in the cabin." *Dalton.* It had to have been. He'd been trying to convince Rein to come up to the café, see what she'd done. So far, that hadn't happened. She stepped forward and grabbed the folder. "Thanks, I'll hang on to it better next time."

"There won't be a next time."

She raised her brow and he continued. "Meaning I'd like you to take over the interior design of the cabins. I admit, I was wrong. You seem to have a very good handle on what I'm looking for."

What an unexpected, pleasant twist. *About damn time.* Liberty studied him. "Yes. Yes, I am." She lifted her mouth in a grin. "But be careful, Slick. Remember what happened last time you tried to make amends." She turned away and in a flash, he stepped across the room and grabbed her arm. His eyes sparkled with a savage glint. She held his gaze, this time he'd have to decide what he wanted.

Obviously, there was a great deal more to this late night

visit than just chatting about her designs. He hadn't figured it out yet, but she had. She'd made up her mind when she saw his heated gaze through the screen door that if she had only one night with him, it would be worth it—for the both of them. Would she get hurt? Probably. But she'd wanted him from the night she climbed in his truck at the bus stop.

His gaze dropped to her mouth and a rush of tingles quickened her body with anticipation. "Was there something else? If not, I'd like to take a shower."

"You know there is, don't you?"

"If by that you mean, like me, you haven't stopped thinking about that kiss or what might have happened if you hadn't stopped? Or that you want to touch me as much as I'm dying to have your hands on me? Then, yes, I do know."

He drew in a sharp breath and closed his eyes, his grasp firm on her arm. "This could get really complicated."

"It doesn't have to be if we both know what we want. If we agree on what it is we need."

His blue eyes bore into her soul. "What do you want, Liberty?"

"I think the real question you have to ask yourself, Rein, is what do you want? We both know you came here for more reason than asking for my help."

"Did I?" He took a step closer, searching her face. "Have you thought about this?" He slid his hands around her waist, his thumbs skimming the hem of her shirt, brushing against her soft flesh. He backed her against the wall and pinned her arms over her head as he pressed his nose to hers. "But you said I wasn't man enough for you."

She searched his gaze, the heat from his body conjuring all manner of seductive images in her head. Her eyes dropped to his tantalizing mouth, remembering the urgency in his kiss and her breasts tightened with need. "So you decided to come over here and prove to me I was wrong?" She could barely catch her breath as he drew closer. "Fine, you win."

The corner of his mouth lifted, showing an irresistible

dimple as his lips hovered over hers. His breath brushed across her skin. "We both win." He captured her mouth then, taking his time, delving into a deep kiss that drugged her senses. Small fires ignited through her, fanned each time his mouth pressed against hers. She tried to fight it—fight him—not wanting to give in.

His lips moved down the curve of her neck, his tongue teasing where her pulse throbbed against her skin. He held her wrists firm, so that she squirmed beneath his grasp, wanting to feel his body and hold it to her. Bracing her hands in one of his, he trailed his finger over her mouth, tracing her lips, drawing a path of fire down her throat, and between the valley of her breasts. He held her gaze, gliding his fingers lightly over her exposed flesh, causing her nipples to pucker through the thin cotton of her shirt. "You asked me what I want." He licked his lips and let his gaze roll over her. "I want to watch you undress."

Liberty swallowed, on the verge of unraveling before him, but she held his heated gaze. "So you want a private show?"

He raised his brow and nodded slowly.

Her heart thrummed. He was already undressing her with his eyes. The thought of being his private dancer was the most erotic thing she'd ever felt. "You know, I'm a hard habit to break." She gave it right back to him. "You'll have a hard time letting go."

"I suspect you're right." He released her hand and stepped back. "As long as we both want the same thing, right?"

She studied his eyes, smoky with desire, then nodded. Taking his hand, she led him to her bedroom. "Sit there."

She stepped into the bathroom and left the door open. In the dim light of her bedside light, she could see him seated on the edge of the bed, his broad shoulders pushed back, and his large hands resting on his knees. There was no need for music, no need for pretense. Enough tension to light a city sizzled between them. She faced him and slowly lifted the camisole over her head. Dangling the shirt midair she kept her eyes fixed on him and let it drop to the floor. She drew her hands over her head and danced, moving her kips to the rhythm playing in her head. With her back to him, she dropped forward, pushing her denim clad bottom up and locked her knees as she swayed side-to-side. Looping her fingers in her back pockets, she faced him, pleased when she heard his sudden intake of air. She repeated the dance, watching her breasts bobbing freely, thinking of his large hands caressing them.

She leaned in the shower and turned on the water, finding a suitable temperature. Spa-like in quality, nothing less would suit Rein. Muted peach and ivory mosaic quartz tile covered the walls. A built-in bench curved into the back corner. The smoky hue of the glass shower doors allowed full view of the bathroom. Every detail had been thoughtfully considered. She glanced over her shoulder and goose bumps rose on her flesh as she imagined what a thorough lover he would be. In one motion, she peeled off her shorts and thong and stepped into the shower. A sound brought her gaze up and he stood inside the door, already barefoot, as he stripped off his shirt and shoved down his jeans.

She'd seen him without a shirt, the view of his chiseled body kept her awake at night, but fully unclothed, she had to force herself to stop staring like some lovesick virgin. She swallowed as he entered the stall and closed the door. Her heart raced as he lifted her face with his fingers, lowering his mouth to hers in a slow, seductive kiss. Her body teetered on the edge of release. The simplicity of his request, the raw hunger in his eyes was enough to arouse her, make her want more. His hands found her waist, drawing her close. "Is this where it gets complicated?" she asked.

"Let's dance." He cupped her face and claimed her mouth. No more seduction. This was, hot, demanding, and possessive. There was no retreat. His firm, calloused hands moved over her body, caressing, teasing, causing heat to pool between her legs. She slid her hand between their bodies, delighting in his quiet moan. He gently covered her hand.

"Not yet, sweetheart," he whispered, bringing her arms up around his neck and kissing her senseless again. "Turn around."

She complied with his request and a moment later felt a cool liquid on her scalp. He slowly massaged the soap through her hair and she leaned into him, closing her eyes, surrendering to his touch. His breath was hot against her neck, his hands filled with lather smoothed over her shoulders, gliding over her skin, cupping her breasts, teasing her firm tips between his fingers. He pressed close, his hard length leaving no illusion of what he offered.

She held her face up to the showerhead, letting the soap slither down her body and his. Holding her against him with one hand, he held a cloth in the other, smoothing it over her triangle of curls and lower between her thighs. He dropped the cloth, continuing to stroke until she purred with satisfaction. She wrapped her arm around his neck, nuzzling the warm, rough underside of his jaw. Her body rocked, grow tight with need. He was more than any fantasy she'd had about him as he took his time to pleasure her, build her desire, to seduce her so completely mind, body and soul. Who'd have thought as much from this stoic, mild-mannered cowboy?

"Is this what you want, Liberty?" he whispered, his teeth raking over her wet flesh. He stroked, finding the spot that brought her to her toes, until her knees grew weak and she crumbled against him, pushing her bottom against him with a ragged sigh.

Growling low, he turned her in his arms. His mouth came down on hers in a fiery kiss that left her unable to breathe. Beneath the stream of water, he held her face in his hands. Water dripped from those impossibly long black eyelashes framing his beautiful eyes. "Protection," he said simply.

"Birth control. I have that covered." She reached out and touched his jaw, drawing him to her, culminating in another heart-stopping kiss. She ached for him, wanted him everywhere, on her, and inside her. He lifted her in his arms, braced her against the wall, and plunged deep. He held her thighs, nestled inside her and met her mouth in a slow, burning kiss. "It's not so complicated, is it?" She smiled and kissed a bead of water from his eyelash.

"Aw, damn," he muttered. "Next time I promise it will be slower."

She wrapped her arms around his neck. "I like fast."

Bodies fused, he moved his powerful hips, filling her with each thrust. She held tight to his neck, her ankles clamped around his waist. Sweet friction, liquid heat pooled between her legs, the tension building as before with mindless desire.

"Look at me," he ordered, his stormy gaze bore into hers.

She clung to him, trying to look at him through the delicious haze swimming in her head, commandeering her body. A soft groan escaped her lips as her body began to crash in a succession of rolling thunder. His gaze narrowed, his mouth set firm and he pushed deep twice more before giving over to his own release.

Swallowing against the dryness in her throat, she blinked, suddenly aware that the water sprayed into her eyes. She swiped at them and met his humorous gaze. "Your water bill is going to be horrific."

The corner of his mouth lifted and he slowly dropped her to her feet. Turning into the water, he forced his hands through his sandy brown hair. He'd probably been a towhead as a child. The thought of him as a young boy sparked an unusual note of sentiment inside her. She noticed then the outline of a bear's claw tattoo on his right shoulder, and the scar it appeared to cover. Liberty traced it with her finger.

He turned and held her face between his hands. His mouth touched hers in a kiss so gentle her body trembled.

"What's the story of that tattoo?" she asked, averting how unprepared she'd been by his kiss.

"Attacked by a bear." He touched his lips to hers, oblivious to her shocked look.

"A real bear?"

He pulled back and smiled. "Pretty much all they have around here."

"How old were you?"

"You realize we're standing here naked in a shower?"

She turned his back to her to get a closer look. "I've never known anyone attacked by a bear and lived through it."

He chuckled and glanced over his shoulder. "I wouldn't have, had Jed not scared him off. We were out hunting, Jed, Michael, and me. When I realized I couldn't outrun the bear, I rolled up in a ball and covered my head."

"That must have been terrifying." She wrapped her arms around his waist and pressed her lips to his shoulder.

"The thought of it still terrifies me. Michael suggested I get the tattoo. He believes because I lived through the attack that the bear and I are brothers now." His hands came over hers. "Tired of my stories?"

She eased her hand lower, amazed to find him partially aroused already. "You distract me."

Turning to face her, he kissed her softly, drawing her mind blank. "I can do better than that."

She snaked her arm around his neck, wanting to taste him again. Her body responded, like oxygen to her soul. She feared she'd never get enough of him. "I believe you can."

"What am I thinking now?" He touched her lips, slow and thorough, setting her skin on fire. He broke the kiss, stepped back and turned off the water.

She took his hand. "I'm hoping you'll show me." She slipped her hand in his and drew him out of the shower stall.

He reached out, tucking a strand of hair behind her ear. "I don't want to hurt you, Liberty. Let's be clear about this before we go any further."

She wouldn't have expected anything less from this man. He said what he felt, honest sometimes to a fault. She might hate herself in the morning, but she'd waited too long—dreamt too many times of him looking at her this way. "I'm a big girl,

Rein. I know what I'm doing." She grabbed a fresh towel and slid it over him, admiring his hard body hewn by rugged work and the outdoors. His bronze skin, even his farmer's tan on his shoulders was sexy. She focused on his firm thighs, and then dropped the towel and looked up at him with a wicked gleam. His hand shot out, smacking the wall for balance as her mouth closed over him.

"Gawd almighty," he said in a broken whisper. "Is that...."

Liberty leaned back. "My tongue stud? What do you think?"

His gaze narrowed as he drew her to her feet, scooped her into his arms, and carried her to the bed. "I think two can play at that game."

Chapter Eight

$\mathcal{R}$ein rubbed his face with the end of his T-shirt and glanced up from his work at Liberty. She stood on a ladder, adjusting a deer horn chandelier she'd picked up at a restoration store in Billings. It couldn't have fit more perfectly with the décor for the rustic cabin. He'd begun to think the same about Liberty. In the weeks they'd worked together, he'd come to realize that she was a voracious self-taught student, researching carefully the history of the area, so she could bring those traditions to life for visitors to the ranch. Talented in many ways and not just in bed, the secret affair that began with the explosive liaison in the shower hadn't weakened. If anything, it'd had gotten to the point where he thought about her on a daily basis, anxiously awaiting for one of their secret "meetings."

He calculated in his head how many such "meetings" they'd had these past few weeks. From a steamy swim in a secluded mountain lake, to sneaking up into the hayloft long after everyone else had gone to bed. They'd even tried out the sturdiness of the old tree-house, deep in the forest glen, that he and his brothers built years ago. He had to remind himself often of their temporary agreement—their summertime fling with no expectations, no strings.

But aside from the off-the-charts passion between them, he found himself savoring the moments when they'd talk about everything—and nothing at all. Those times when she'd curl up under his arm and fall asleep. She was a giving lover, aware of what pleased him. They joked about feeling like kids, having that freedom, the secret thrill of being caught. It made their times together all the more enticing.

She tipped the light, checked the fixture, and glanced at him. "What do you think?"

Standing on that ladder in those shorts and a skimpy pink tee shirt would at one time caused him to be critical of how she dressed, now he didn't see her clothes at all, knowing intimately what a wonderland existed beneath.

"Beautiful." He removed his tool belt and snaked his way through the disarray of furniture waiting to be arranged in the great room. During the course of the past few weeks, with Liberty taking care of the esthetics, the cabin project had been moving along much faster than expected, of the six cabins Rein had planned on this project. He already had four complete and a fifth, nearly done.

She smiled watching him. "Smooth talker."

"Come on down here, I'll show you smooth."

Raising her brow, Liberty descended the ladder, turning to face him on the last rung. "It's the middle of the day. Aren't you afraid someone will discover us?"

Rein couldn't be sure whether Dalton suspected the two were having an affair. He never asked, but he'd chosen to remain up at the main house after Wyatt and Aimee returned from their honeymoon. Rein had chosen not to ask why. Wyatt, on the other hand, preoccupied with Aimee, the pregnancy, and getting the nursery ready, had hardly asked about the cabins at all.

Rein lifted the hem of her shirt, seeing her smooth skin, now browned by working outside, driving him crazy at times in wearing her shorts and a swimsuit top. He pressed his face to her flesh, inching his mouth up her torso, pleased when she clamped her hands on the ladder for balance. He wanted her undone, just as she'd become an addiction for him.

Barely a week had gone by all summer that they hadn't found somewhere to meet in private. Nights when they all gathered at the main house and he played cards with his brothers, he'd look over to find her shooting him a smile meant to invite him later to her bed. On occasion, he'd make the excuse of having to go with her on a buying trip to Billings, and most often they'd find an isolated hotel room on the edge of town for a few hours.

"Dalton's gone to Billings. Wyatt's rubbing Aimee's feet and watching chick flicks this afternoon." He breathed in her sweet scent of coconut and vanilla, gently raking his teeth across her flesh.

She smoothed her fingers through his hair. "Then we have some time. What you'd have in mind?" He glanced up at her and grinned.

"Driving you crazy." He grew hard just thinking of what he wanted to do to her, to feel her hands on his body, to hear her soft groan like always when they came together. They'd agreed that they both wanted the companionship for as long as it lasted and when the time to part ways, there'd be no regrets. He searched her dark eyes and tried not to get sucked in—by her beauty, her honesty. She didn't belong here. Eventually it wouldn't be enough. Like Caroline, it was fun, but in the end, she'd leave him for the bright lights and big city.

He unsnapped her shorts and drew both down her shapely thighs. She wrapped her arms around his neck. "You just lean back, relax."

"Glad this isn't a wooden ladder." She flashed him a smile.

He brushed his unshaven cheek against her soft flesh.

She leaned back, a proverbial banquet of his lust. Her dark eyes invited him—no challenged him—to make her scream. And he intended to do just that. It'd become a game of wits to out-pleasure one another. He'd done things, made love in places he'd never dreamt of. She was unconventional, encouraging him to be adventurous, and try new things in and out of bed. It fueled his creativity, took him outside the comfort zone he'd built around himself after Caroline left him.

Her skin was warm, her musky scent heady as he lifted her leg over his shoulder. He closed his mouth over her...tasting and teasing. Her fingers dug into his hair, tightening with the building of her climax. Her heel dug into his shoulder, her soft cries driving him to the brink. The ladder rocked against the floor. The desire to claim her, to know every part of her body, drove his need.

"Oh, Rein." His name rolling off her tongue in a reverent whisper, nearly undid him. She sighed and with a smile, slid into his embrace covering his mouth in a sensuous kiss. He eased her to the floor. These days he carried protection at all times. Though she'd said indicated she took the pill he felt compelled to be as responsible for as often as they were together.

It was like that, one minute they were working on a project, the next unable to keep their hands off each other. She'd become a drug he needed daily—whether kissing her tempting mouth, making love and feeling her give as much as take, or bouncing around ideas on décor. The more time they'd spent together the more he'd found to admire. As much as he refused to believe that he could be falling for her, he had a hard time picturing her with another man. But he'd reserved those ideas, kept them to himself, not wanting to hear her remind him that they agreed to something temporary, that one day she'd leave him, leave the ranch.

"We've never done it on the floor." She smiled drawing him into the warm, cradle of her thighs, taunting him before he could get his jeans down. A cough outside the cabin, and the crunch of gravel brought them both upright. Liberty scrambled into her shorts and stood. Rein, on his knees, grabbed a box and pretended to be helping unpack a lamp just as the front door opened.

"You guys in here?" Wyatt stuck his head inside and looked around.

"Hey," Liberty said, her voice shook a bit. Or maybe Rein's

guilt at nearly being caught imagined it. Liberty turned away, pretending to unwrap a lampshade.

"Hey, thought chick flicks were on the agenda today?" Rein offered a friendly grin.

"Yeah, that was the plan. Fortunately, Aimee fell asleep on the couch. So I thought I'd sneak down here and see how things are going. Don't tell her, but those movies about drive me nuts." He stepped further into the room and surveyed the surroundings. "It's looking good, guys."

Rein and Liberty remained frozen in place.

Wyatt glanced over, his expression curious. "You two, okay?"

"Uh, just a bit of a scare, really. Liberty nearly fell off the ladder. But we're okay...she's okay. You okay, Liberty?" He glanced over his shoulder.

"Yep, I'm good. Good thing you were here though. That could have been a nasty fall." She scooted past Rein, and made a bee-line for the kitchen. "Think maybe I need some water. Either of you need anything?"

With any luck, Wyatt bought the BS they were shoveling at him. His gaze followed Liberty before darting back to Rein. "No, thanks, I'm good." His steady gaze remained on Rein. "Say, Aimee wanted me to ask if you'd like to go into Billings with her tomorrow. She wanted to pick up a few more things for the baby's room." He called out.

"Okay with me, providing boss man will let me go." She peeked around the corner with a smile.

Wyatt's brow crooked as he continued to stare at Rein.

Clearing his throat, he averted his brother's questioning look, choosing physical excursion to redirect his curiosity. "Help me move this sofa into place, Wyatt." He waited as he picked up the other end of the couch. "You think it's wise for Aimee to travel?" Damn thing weighed a ton, but if it took that to flush the lascivious thoughts from his brain, then so be it.

That one look from Wyatt was a two-by-four reality check to his head. He and Liberty were both consenting adults, true, but it'd been a long time since Rein had kept any secrets from either of his brothers. He had a gut feeling that Wyatt had caught on to their little secret and he was about to find out how he felt about it. Hell, he wasn't sure if he could explain how he felt about Liberty. Rein trudged forward, trying to avoid the obvious. "She's getting to be as big as a barn." Damn. Too much honesty.

Wyatt dropped his end of the couch and Rein followed, missing his toe by a slim margin.

"I meant that in a good way. You guys sure you're not having twins?" Rein attempted to recover from his faux pas. Wyatt's expression eased a little. He plopped down on the couch and wearily brushed his hand through his dark hair. "Yeah, I wondered the same thing. Doc swears there's only one in there. Apparently, he's just a big boy."

"A boy?" This was the first that Wyatt had revealed this news, at least to him. He held his hand out to shake his brother's hand. "Another Kinnison male. That's terrific, Wyatt."

"Thanks." Wyatt gave him a shaky smile. I'm a little worried about Aimee. She's such a tiny thing. Seems like lately, she's tired all the time and her ankles...." He shook her head. "I've delivered a lot of horses in my day. But I don't know how to make her comfortable."

"Women have been having babies since the dawn of time, Wyatt," Liberty stated as she leaned against the kitchen doorway. "Aimee's a smart, capable woman. She's done everything right. It's going to be fine."

"I hope you're right," Wyatt responded.

"Of course, I am. You'll see. Okay boys," Liberty said. "Think I'll run up and see what time she wants to head into Billings."

As soon as the door closed behind her, Wyatt's gaze slammed into Rein's. "What's going on?"

Though Rein anticipated the question, he still wasn't entirely certain how best to answer it. What had begun as a little harmless fun had escalated into something that Rein couldn't explain. "I'm not sure what you mean," Rein said. His futile attempt at stalling not appreciated by Wyatt.

Wyatt's shot him an incredulous look. "Are you serious? You forget I haven't had sex in...." He pressed his fingers to his brow. "I-I can't even remember. You think though I don't recognize that kind of tension when I see it?"

Rein stuffed his hands in his pockets. He couldn't lie—he wouldn't—not to Wyatt. "Okay, we've been...seeing each other."

"*Seeing* each other?" Wyatt eyed him, stood and braced his hand on the mantel. "As in the biblical sense?"

Rein grimaced at the reference. "Really? Call it like it is."

"Yeah, like you should be preaching to me. You're sleeping with Liberty? You're sleeping with *my sister*."

"Half-sister, not that it makes a difference, and yes." He paused and blew out a breath. "We mutually consented to this. She is a grown woman."

"I don't think I want to hear this."

Rein shrugged. "You did ask."

"And why didn't you mention this to anyone?"

"For this very reason. We didn't feel it was anybody's business but our own. I won't lie. I don't think either of us knows yet what we want, but we've got things under control. We both know what we're doing."

Maybe he wanted to believe that her passion could carry over enough to keep her here. But he'd made that mistake once before and had his heart broken. He couldn't make himself believe he could love like that ever again and even if he did discover he'd fallen for her, Liberty had made it clear that once the baby was born and the cabins were complete, she'd thought she'd go back to school and pursue a career in design.

"Under control, huh?" Wyatt folded his arms over his chest as he faced Rein. "And do you love her?"

"Does Dalton love every woman he's ever slept with? Did you, before Aimee?" Rein tried to avoid the question.

"We're not talking about that, we're talking about my little sister."

Maybe this was best to have it out in the open. Keeping a secret had become a burden and though he'd been honest with Liberty, he hadn't been with his Wyatt and Dalton. Still, this relationship between him and Liberty—regardless of anyone else's opinion—was still theirs and they would determine the outcome. Rein blinked as he realized where his thoughts had taken him.

When had this thing between them become a relationship? The truth hit him that he well might be falling for this girl and did she even know it? How would she take such news?

"So what you're saying is that you've seen each other a few times, but it's nothing exclusive, right? If you want to see other people, or if she does, you're both okay with that?" Wyatt countered.

He'd been focused on Liberty long before they slept together. He'd just been denying the attraction, tossing every possible excuse in the road to try to detour his thoughts. He couldn't speak for Liberty, of course. She was young, but wise beyond her years. He doubted that would make much difference to Wyatt. "I'm not seeing anyone else, I don't know about Liberty. If she wants to see other men, I won't stop her." He kept a steady gaze on Wyatt hoping that it didn't show that he'd just lied through his teeth.

"That's bullshit and you know it. How do you feel about her, Rein?"

Rein released a sigh. "I care for her...a lot. But neither of us is blind to reality. She doesn't plan to stay here, and I have no plans to leave. So, there it is."

An awkward silence stretched between them. Wyatt's tended to be more of a black and white kind of guy, as opposed to an it-could-go-either-way-type guy.

"Jesus Criminy, Rein. Are you serious?" He threw out a short laugh and turned away. "She's my little sister."

"And a grown woman," Rein reminded him. "I'm not alone

in this decision. It's what she wanted, too."

"What she wanted?" Wyatt dismissed him with his hand. "You're sure about that?"

"It's not interfering with anything. The cabins are coming along fine...better, in fact since she's been helping me." A weak reason, but worth tossing out there.

"Pretty damn convenient then, isn't it, having her working alongside you?"

"It's not like that, Wyatt." Rein found himself defending the doubts that had niggled at the back of his brain, too dazed by his desire and her willingness to look at things realistically. "She's very good at what she does."

"Oh, I just bet," he retorted in a caustic tone.

"You know what I mean. Look around. She's done an amazing job."

Wyatt's face was grim. "Yep, it is amazing what a person will do when they're strung along. You forget I grew up hoping to please someone by doing whatever she asked of me. Moving from one deadbeat hotel to another, sleeping in a car, every damn day hoping she'd wake up and reciprocate that love. Instead, she walked out of our lives, leaving us to pick up the pieces."

"I'm not like your mom, Wyatt. I'm not stringing her—" Bile rose in his throat. He couldn't finish the comment. "That was never my intent. I wanted her to work with me. Hell, you're the one who suggested it. The rest, well...it just happened. I don't know what else to say."

"And you really think she's not going to get hurt? When the cabins are done and there's no more for her to do around here for you? You think she's just going to walk away from this unscathed?"

He wanted to believe Wyatt didn't understand, that his judgment had been affected by the poor experiences he'd had with women in his past. But his sister was nothing like those women. She was like no woman he'd ever known— fiercely independent, she was determined to make it and on her own terms. She'd not surrendered to him. They'd surrendered to each other, taking and giving what the other needed. They'd not intended for it to be exclusive; but somehow it had turned out that way. Or had it? Had he been blind to her attentiveness? A soft smile delivered across the family table at dinner, or the way she managed to sit next to him when they gathered around the fire pit at night, and listened to Michael tell his stories of the Crow tribes.

Then there were the stolen moments where they were animals in heat, unable to quench their sexual thirst. "I think you may be wrong, Wyatt. But honestly, I hadn't thought about it."

"Damn right you haven't. You've been thinking with your dick and little else, it sounds like. Seems to me, one of you better give it some thought."

He wanted to defend himself, wanted to justify that he and Liberty were adults and didn't owe anyone an explanation. But if what Wyatt said was true, if Liberty had agreed to the arrangement because she hoped for, expected more...?

Somewhere, deep inside, he'd compared her to Caroline, justifying to himself that she had other plans, she didn't care about the ranch or about him. Like him, she'd wanted to keep things simple, have a good time. But maybe he'd selfish, been blinded by his own experience, because in truth, Liberty was nothing at all like Caroline. Maybe Wyatt was right. Maybe he'd been lying to himself, convinced that she knew what she was doing, so that he wouldn't have to think that he might be using her.

He faced Wyatt's stern expression. "You're right. Though it's the Gods truth I never intended to hurt her. I made it clear I'm not interested in any long term relationship. She agreed. I believed her, or maybe I wanted to." Rein glanced at Wyatt and realized that he needed to have a serious talk with Liberty and the sooner, the better. He had no idea of the repercussions, but like it or not, he'd have to end things now, before the situation got out of hand. "I'll take care of it,

Wyatt."

"Unless you plan to make an honest woman of her, I suggest you do so, before she gets hurt."

Rein watched his brother leave. He cared for her, he did. But they'd known from the beginning eventually they'd part ways. After his talk with Wyatt, he had a sick feeling that maybe he might already too late.

☙

Rein had managed to keep himself scarce since Wyatt surprised them the day before. He hadn't shown up for dinner, nor had he knocked on her patio door as had become the custom. It had shaken them both, but perhaps Rein, more so. If he'd confided to his brother about the fact they were seeing each other, Wyatt may have made him realize that despite his claims of mutual consent, the fact that they'd not seen anyone since their affair started might have scared Rein.

Maybe it was better this way. She needed to take a break from him. Working together on a daily basis, sharing his ideas, listening to him talk about the future of this project after they'd made love had caused her to carve out a niche in her heart solely for him. It had been a dangerous thing to realize and then accept, but she'd convinced herself she'd had to let go of relationships before and though, for a time, there'd be heartache, this would be no different.

There'd been a time or two that she'd wanted to spill her guts and tell him that she thought she might be falling for him, but the thought of his reaction should she renege on their agreement was enough to keep her thoughts to herself. Instead, she found ways to show him how much she cared and respected him. Not only in small ways, but in the how she trusted him in bed, allowing their fantasies to unfold without restraint.

God, she thought. He was an amazing lover, exciting and experimental, yet thoughtful of her pleasure as much as his own. It was no great surprise then, when she realized she'd fallen hard for him.

"What do you think of this?" Aimee held up a light blue one-piece romper.

Liberty blinked from her reverie, the image of Rein in her bed vanishing in a quick poof. She focused on the umpteenth romper they'd looked at today. It had a sheriff's badge sewn to the breast and fabric printed boots for the feet. Starting in when the stores opened, they'd been to three different baby boutiques in Billings, averaging over an hour in each. Liberty's stomach growled plaintively. She shifted the bags in her arms and smiled. The woman had bought at least one of everything that had tickled her fancy. At this rate, the kid would grow out of them faster than he'd be able to wear them.

"It's adorable, like everything else you've bought today." Liberty held up the bags. "You do realize if you continue to buy everything, there will be nothing left for the shower Betty wants to give you after the baby's born."

Aimee shot her a pained grin. "I know, but I can't help it. I keep seeing him in all these cute little clothes."

Liberty sighed. "Yeah, fair enough. You make your decision, I'm going to go drop these in the truck and feed the meter. After that, we're going to get you off your feet for a bit and have some lunch. Wyatt will have my head if you come home with swollen ankles."

Aimee smiled. A faint blush tinged her cheeks. "He's been amazing through this. He's shown the patience of a saint with my mother's incessant calling to see how I'm doing, or if there's been any change." Her eyes welled with her wobbly smile.

"Oh, no, don't start with the waterworks, girlfriend." Liberty blinked and sucked in a deep breath. The thought flashed in her mind, of how Eloise would've taken the news of becoming a grandmother. Not nearly as graciously as Aimee's folks, she guessed.

"I'm very fortunate he'll have aunts and uncles and

grandparents to be close to. I think that's the best present this little guy is going to get." She patted her ever-growing tummy. She tipped her head, regarding Liberty. "I've been meaning to ask, have you had a chance to talk to your brothers about the letter that your mom wrote to them, but never sent?"

She shrugged. "There hasn't really been a good time. I'm not sure it's as important to them as I thought it once might be. Jed did an amazing job all on his own it seems. I think mom knew all along that he would. She had been searching for her piece of the pie and thought my father could give it to her. He can be very convincing when he wants to be." She shook her head, dispelling the image of her last conversation with her father. "At any rate, I've never met men like Wyatt, Dalton, and Rein. There like these guys you read about in books—self-made, loyal, hard-working, gentlemen with a soft spot for babies and animals." She chuckled. "Modern day cowboys in the flesh."

Aimee listened, her eyes studying Liberty. She hooked the little blue sleeper over her arm and thumbed through the others hanging nearby. "I'm glad that Rein came to his senses about asking you to work with him on the cabins. I can't believe how fast things have progressed."

Liberty averted her eyes from Aimee's studious gaze. "Amazing, isn't it, that we've managed to get so much accomplished and not kill each other in the process."

She smiled. "It seems to me he's not nearly as edgy around you as he used to be. And you don't appear quite as frustrated with him, either."

Liberty sensed where the conversation was leading. She wasn't prepared, however to get into it with Aimee or anyone, just yet. "Yeah, I guess we both accepted each other for the way we are." She didn't miss the curious glint in Aimee's eye and wondered if Dalton, perhaps, had expressed his thoughts to Wyatt and Aimee. Why otherwise would Dalton left her drawings where Rein would find them? Then again, the plan could have been purely platonic, intended to entice Rein to see and use her skills and accept her help on the cabins. Simple. Her concern about how her brothers would view the steamy little affair had been burning in her gut since Wyatt surprised her and Rein yesterday. "I'm just glad that he finally got it through that stubborn head of his that I'm good for something."

The comment, meant to be flippant, conjured instead times when she and Rein were alone. He was a man of strength, raw, rugged and yet, he gave her freedom in bed, sharing equally the pleasuring. Nothing brought her undone faster than seeing his face upturned, his eyes closed, lost in a guttural moan of pure pleasure and know that she'd played a role in that. The mere thought made her wet, increasing her frustration.

She hadn't seen or spoken to him since Wyatt's visit and it tore her up inside wanting to know what transpired between them. "You go ahead and finish here. I'll wait by the truck. There's a cute little café across the street that has great salads."

Aimee shot her a look. "Have you been to Billings for lunch without me?" Having the summer off as a teacher and being pregnant had made Aimee restless. She'd read every book on raising children, watched tons of sappy romance movies, and tried to learn to knit, something she'd started to teach herself last winter. But given the chance to get out, she jumped all over that. Thus far, none of it had quenched her restlessness like shopping.

"It must have been one of those times I came into Billings on a buying trip with Rein. We grabbed a bite to eat, I guess."

"You guess." She smiled, with an unmistakable twinkle in her eye. "Okay, go on, I'll be out in a minute."

Relieved to escape Aimee's thinly veiled and estrogen-charged scrutiny, Liberty walked out of the store and took a deep breath. They'd been lucky enough to find metered parking in the middle of the block, allowing easy access to the stores Aimee had wanted to visit.

Liberty slipped the bags in the backseat of the cab and fished in her pocketbook for more change. She loved this weather. The sky stretched blue and cloudless overhead. Sunny and warm for late summer, a nip of fall hung the air. She glanced down the street as she deposited money enough for another two hours, noting the brightly colored pink and purple petunias hanging on every lamppost. She enjoyed the small-town atmosphere, compared to the twenty-four hustle and bustle of Vegas. People here said "hello", they seemed friendlier, happier, it seemed. More content. She tried to imagine herself in such a place, settling down, taking some classes and perhaps starting her own interior design business.

Her gaze drifted across the street hoping to find room yet at one of the quaint little outside tables of the café, especially during the business lunch hour. She straightened, her eyes narrowing on a man seated at one of the tables. The sun overhead and the newspaper he perused shielded the details of his face. Liberty found herself staring and when he turned the page, a gasp tore from her throat. She recognized one of Angelo's men, reading a newspaper and having coffee as though he belonged there. *What was Franco doing in Billings?*

"Ready?"

Startled, she whirled to face Aimee and dropped the coins, sending them all over the sidewalk.

"You look like you've seen a ghost. Are you all right?"

Liberty bent down and quickly scooped up the change. When she straightened again, she darted a look across the street, finding the table where he'd been empty. She quickly scanned the area and immediately thought of Elaina, realizing how long it'd been since she spoke to her last. Then again, she'd been far too preoccupied to notice until now. She slapped herself mentally for thinking Angelo would let her walk away with repercussion. As soon as she got home, she needed to contact her friend.

"Liberty?"

She met Aimee's questioning look. "Yeah?"

"Are you okay? All the color has drained from your face."

She blinked and attempted a smile to dismiss her uneasy feelings. "Sure, just a bit light-headed. Let's get some lunch."

CR

Rein was in town discussing plumbing issues with Tyler when she and Aimee returned late afternoon. Relieved when Aimee said she wanted to sneak in a nap before dinner, it gave Liberty a good excuse to deposit her at the main house and hurry down to her cabin where she could contact Elaina.

Safely tucked inside, she couldn't shake the odd feeling of being watched. Only Angelo could have sent Franco, but for what purpose? Why wouldn't he simply confront her? Angelo certainly had reason to be angry with her, but why now, after all this time?

She picked up her new cellphone and saw a number of texts from her friend, all in the last twenty-four hours. Liberty kicked herself for not checking her phone earlier and her concerns were no less relieved as she scanned through the messages.

Angelo found out about the ranch. He spoke to your dad, who told him you might have gone to see your half-brothers place in Montana. Thought you should know.

She read the next message:

Angelo called me tonight. He said if I didn't verify where you were, he'd make sure I never danced again. I'm scared, Libby. What do I tell him?

Liberty's stomach roiled with fear. Angelo had a bad temper, but when high, out of his mind, he was capable of anything. He'd gone straight to her father—that made matters worse. Her father had a number of unsavory connections. The two working together, could mean that if she stuck around, her family might be in danger. Even now they could be. They'd all accepted her, despite her strange past, yet what would any of them think to know that her father was abetting her ex-boyfriend, an addict and probable drug dealer, to locate her.

She walked to the back door, and searched the twilight purple sky she'd come to love for an answer. But tonight, the dusky shadows were not as serene. She felt alone, isolated. The thick pine forest a few yards from her back door appeared ominous...unfriendly. She checked the lock on the patio door and closed the curtains to block the view.

A knock startled her and she had to stop a moment to remember that Franco wouldn't likely waltz up to her front door. She peeked out the front window and to her relief saw Dalton. He waved as she dropped the curtain. Taking a deep breath, she opened the door and forced a smile. "Hey."

"Hey, yourself. I see you survived shopping with our sister-in-law." He glanced at her. She saw a puzzled glint flicker through his dark eyes. "I had to get something out of the one of the cabins, so I thought I'd stop by and tell you that supper is almost ready." She knew he was stalling, watching her. "You feel okay? You look kinda pasty."

She waved off his comment. "Aw, just a little tired. Rein has been getting me up early these days."

"The boy does like his sunrises." He smiled. "Come on, dinner will make you feel better." He put his hand on the doorknob.

"Is Rein home yet?"

Her brother stopped, thinking a moment before he spoke. "No, he's not back yet. That's weird. He knew Wyatt planned on fixing one of his steak dinners tonight. He never misses those. Guess his mind is on other things these days. But I don't need to tell you that, do I?" He chuckled.

Liberty's eyes grew wide. Did he know about them, then?

"Because, like you said, he's getting up earlier?" He peered at her. "You sure you feel okay?"

She couldn't explain anything until she'd spoken to Rein. If the time had come to reveal their relationship to the family, then they should do so together. Right now, of greater concern were Rein's safety and whereabouts, as well as her family's safety. Her phone vibrated, indicating another text. Dalton glanced at the phone. "Maybe that's Rein?"

Not likely. She hadn't seen or heard anything from Rein in over twenty-four hours. She checked the message. "Nah, it's just a friend back home." She met Dalton's eyes. "Uh, back in Vegas."

He smiled and his eyes sparkled with an acceptance that made Liberty happy and sad at the same time. She liked Dalton. She'd discovered that they were in some ways alike, enjoying many of the same things. Their common rebellious attitude for instance made her realize that Vegas was no longer her home. *This* was home. These people were her family. She had to do what she could to protect them.

"Well, when you're done, come on up and get some dinner. We'll keep it warm."

She nodded as he left, then she tapped to check the new text on her phone.

Call me as soon as you can. Urgent.

In haste, Liberty called, her stomach clenched as she waited through more than three rings. *Where was Rein? Why isn't Elaina answering her phone?*

"Libby?" Her friend finally answered, but she sounded frightened.

"What's the matter, Elaina? Are you all right?"

A brief moment of silence ticked by and then a male came on the line. "Hello, my darling. You left without saying goodbye."

She froze at the sound of Angelo's voice.

"I'd ask if you missed me, but I'm told that it appears you've settled right in with your new family. Your mother would be pleased. I can't say as much for your father."

"What do you want?" A cold dread settled in her stomach. She held the edge of the table, easing slow onto the dining room chair.

"For starters, I'd like my star dancer back, of course.

You're costing me, love. Our regulars want to see Liberty Belle. Poor Elaina. She's tried, but she's not you."

"You leave her alone and you leave me alone. I don't owe you anything." She leveled a warning slow and easy. He was with Elaina and if anything happened to her, Liberty would never forgive herself.

"Oh, now see that's where your memory seems a little shaky. As I remember it, I took you from a dead-end waitress job, set you up in one of my penthouse suites and damn near gave you everything you ever owned."

She couldn't deny it. But she'd been sucked in by him, charmed by his confidence and veiled promises—much like her mother had been. But, she wasn't her mother and she had a choice. She appealed to his wallet. "I can send you the money for the cut I didn't pay you on my last check. I can send you installments for the back rent I owe you for the apartment."

His low chuckle, infused with evil, made the hair on the back of her neck stand on end. "Tell you what. Why don't you come on back home and we'll sit down and talk this out."

It wasn't an option and they both knew it "Did you send Franco here to bring me back?" she challenged. "Franco? I don't know what you're talking about." The innocent tone in his voice made her want to throw up. He knew damn well that she understood he'd sent Franco as a guarantee he meant business. He held all the cards. She had no choice but to comply until she could figure out what to do.

"If I come back, will you swear to leave Elaina alone?" The very idea turned her stomach, but she'd do it if he agreed to leave her family and friends alone.

"You're in no position to bargain here, Liberty. I'm being a nice guy. Don't make me change my mind about that."

She hesitated, wanting to unleash the anger building inside of her. Why hadn't she seen his controlling ways, so like her father? "Okay." She kept her voice steady to appease him. "You win. I'll head back tonight."

"Good. I'm giving you two hours to let me know when to

send a car to pick you up at the airport. Don't be late."

"Fine."

"Liberty?"

"What." She stood and walked to the bedroom where began tossing her things on the bed.

"If I don't hear from you in a couple of hours with your flight information, I'm afraid things are going to get much worse, not only for Elaina, but for the rest of your family as well. Do we have an understanding?"

He made it clear she shouldn't try to run and disappear.

"Yes, I understand perfectly."

"Good." He paused. "I've missed you, my love."

The line went dead not allowing her the chance to respond. She stared at the phone, her head swirling with the number of ways she'd like to rid the world of this slime-bag. She'd always thought of herself as a survivor, unafraid, perhaps too trusting of a warm smile and handsome face. She knew now that a man's charm lasted only long enough to get what they wanted.

Maybe that's why Rein was being so evasive. Whatever the brothers had discussed had apparently made quite the impression. But she couldn't speculate about what happened between them just now. She had to take her life back. She wouldn't run away this time, wouldn't spend her days looking over her shoulder. If he wanted a fight, she'd give him one to remember and bring the police along for the ride. She'd be only too happy to share with them some of the shady dealings she'd seen while working at the club.

As for Rein, he'd made it clear that what they had was purely physical. She'd wanted him as much as he wanted her. It was her fault that she allowed her heart to get in the way, to believe that this cowboy would ride her off into the sunset and a happily ever after. Reality was a bitch, but she'd make it, she'd survived plenty of heartache in her life, and she would again. But, first, she needed to make sure that Angelo would never bother her family and friends again.

Chapter Nine

*R*ein hesitated, his fist poised to knock on Liberty's door. Deep down, he'd known that they'd have to have this conversation, even though part of him had hoped they wouldn't need to. Wyatt was right. He knew it The charade they'd been playing couldn't go on forever and if pretending that it could deceived Liberty into thinking there was more between them, then it had to end. She was an amazing, exceptional woman and he couldn't deny together in bed, it was off the charts. But neither of them had held any expectations that it would last. On the upside, and hopefully it would make things easier, they'd never made any declarations to one another. No promises, even in the height of passion. And that was a good thing, wasn't it?

Rein learned long ago to reserve his heart for things he could count on—family, nature, building things with his hands. He'd also learned that a woman's word was only as good as the next offer that might come along. With her talent and her beauty, it wouldn't be long before Liberty had a hundred guys vying for her attention, offering her a life, more exciting, more fulfilling than what he could give her on the ranch.

He wanted that—wanted the very best for her. He didn't want to hold her back from growing, finding her potential.

Though eight years difference in age didn't seem like much now, would it down the road? Would she come to resent him? He couldn't do that to her. However much it pained him to let her go now, it was better than experiencing heartbreak down the road.

He paused, hearing her raised voice. Her tone sounded urgent. With a frown, he knocked on the door and a few moments went by before she finally opened it.

"Oh, it's you." She swung open the door, holding the phone to her ear, clearly preoccupied. He glanced at the phone.

"Is this a bad time?"

She blinked, her face dissolving into a smile as though she'd just realized his presence.

"May I come in?"

No kiss hello. No warm hugs. But her smile stay plastered on her face as she nodded and walked into the living room, leaving him to enter on his own. "Is everything okay?" She seemed lost in her thoughts. Maybe Wyatt had already spoken to her.

"Uh, yeah." She straightened her shoulders and faced him. "Everything's fine now that you're here." She walked over, dropping her phone on the coffee table. And just like that, she seemed back to her old self. She ran her palms over his chest. "Seems you've been a busy boy. I missed you last night. Look what I ordered online." She picked up and shook a small brown box, then pulled out a pair of fur-lined cuffs from inside. "Thought we might play a little cops and robbers." She twirled them on her finger. "Internet shopping is so easy."

Rein looked at her. She'd gone from being on another planet, to seducing him in record time. Visions of being handcuffed to her headboard caused his entire body to come alive. Quelled as quickly by her sudden change in demeanor and the urgency he'd heard in her voice. He sensed she was keeping something from him. Yet another reason they needed to get everything on the table.

"Listen I came by because we need to discuss a few

things." He took her hand and led her to the couch. Carefully inching away when she tried to snuggle with him. He'd never be able to do this if he allowed her too close. There was no easy way to say what he had to tell her.

"Wyatt knows."

She stared at him, a questioning gaze in her dark brown eyes. Eyes he'd seen fill with the heat of desire when they made love. She blinked as reality hit her. Her eyes widened.

"You mean, he knows...about us?"

Rein nodded. "Yeah." He all but heard the gears rolling in her beautiful head.

"How'd that go?"

"About like you'd expect."

Her face clouded. "I'm old enough to make my own choices. It's really none of his or anyone else's business. What matters is the agreement we made, right? Although I have to say, I'm surprised you didn't wait until we were both present to talk about this with Wyatt."

He understood and maybe it would have been better had she been there, but he doubted Wyatt would have been as free to say what he had. Besides, it's not like they were ready to make some grand announcement about their relationship.

There was that word again.

He studied her face, realizing he knew every freckle, knew where she was ticklish, and knew what made her sigh. Hell, what had he been thinking? He took her hands in his. "You know I never wanted this to get complicated. I never wanted to hurt you, I still don't."

She squeezed his hands. "I know what I agreed to, Rein. I've never had any illusions."

Her words stabbed at a small piece of his heart. Thus far he'd been able to keep his emotions out of the equation. "We need to take some time to think about what we're doing. No more secrets, somebody's bound to get hurt, maybe not today, but eventually."

"Meaning when it's time for me to leave?" She held his

gaze.

Part of him desperately wanted her to say she'd come to love the ranch. That she'd found something here that made her content, but he had no intention of risking that assumption again. *Fool me once*—had become his philosophy.

He swallowed. "Maybe it's better this way." He rubbed his thumb over the back of her delicate hands, hands that had touched his body, driven him to delirious insanity. Already a hole had formed in his gut. He'd done the one thing he'd sworn he wouldn't do again—he'd gotten too close. Better to end this now on a pre-emptive strike, than for either of them to suffer the consequences later.

She glanced at him, released a quick sigh, and let go of his grasp. Pushing quickly to her feet, she scooped up her phone as she walked toward the door. "If you'll excuse me, I have a few things I need to take care of."

Of all the reactions, he imagined, her total lack of concern surprised him. She opened the front door and waited for him to leave. Confused by her sudden mood changes, he hesitated a moment then rose to leave. Hadn't this been what he wanted? A clean break? It seemed pretty clear to him, anyway that Wyatt's assessment of her had been terribly off. While Rein knew all the reasons that they should end this affair before someone got hurt, he hadn't expected the undeniable ache in his heart. "You're okay, then?" He reached out to touch her shoulder and she inched back.

"Absolutely. I think it's better this way—like you said."

"No regrets." He reiterated the mantra of the glorious secret they'd shared between them all summer.

"None." She held his gaze. Her phone rang and she glanced at the caller. "If you'll excuse me, I need to take this."

"Sure." He stepped outside and turned to say he'd see her at dinner, but the door had already been closed. And just like that she'd shut him out of her life.

C3

With Dalton doing chores, and Aimee checking her purchases from the day, Rein found himself helping Wyatt clear the supper dishes. Liberty hadn't showed up, calling Aimee to tell her that she'd started a project she needed to finish and not to hold supper.

"You get a chance to talk to Liberty?" Wyatt rinsed off another plate and placed it in the dishwasher.

Rein glumly stuffed leftovers into plastic containers, setting them in the fridge. The fact that she'd not shown for dinner bothered him. And while he hadn't expected cartwheels about their break-up, he couldn't shake the feeling that something else seemed wrong. Maybe it was nothing more than his badly bruised ego. The fact that she'd been able to quickly end the affair made him feel guilty, angry, and confused. Hell, he didn't know what to think. "Yeah," he answered. "It's for certain that your concerns about Liberty's feelings were severely misguided, in fact, she took the news much better than I'd expected."

Wyatt looked at Rein, and then continued loading the dishwasher.

"She's never talked much about her past, has she?"

Wyatt raised a brow and shook his head. "Nope. I know she and Aimee have talked a little bit. Mainly girl talk stuff, I'd guess." Wyatt stopped, leaned against the counter and crossed his arms. He looked at Rein. "So, what did she say?"?"

Rein closed the refrigerator door and stared at the family pictures Aimee had started to attach to the surface with magnets. There was the whole group taken at the wedding, with Wyatt and Aimee on the horse, the rest of the family surrounding them. He thought of that night. The first time he'd kissed Liberty and how from that moment he couldn't seem to get enough of her. "To be honest, she seemed totally fine with ending things between us. Guess maybe it didn't mean as much as I thought it might. Kind of strange." He shrugged.

"Rein?"

He faced his brother. A myriad of thoughts assaulted him. So much had changed since that happy group picture. He and Aimee were expecting a child in a few weeks. With Liberty's help, the cabins were nearly finished and would be ready to rent by next spring.

"Rein, did you want it to mean something to her?"

The question gave him pause to consider what it was he wanted. He lifted his shoulders. "I don't know. We had fun. She's a beautiful, amazing woman."

"Enough." Wyatt shot him a pointed look. "I don't need to hear details." His gaze narrowed and an odd smile formed on his lips. "Maybe the thing you should be asking, is did this mean something more to you? More than you want to admit?"

Oh, Rein had thought about it. Each time they made love and listened to her sleeping softly in the crook of his arm. He didn't want to face the reality that he'd not been able to keep his side of the bargain...that somewhere along the way he'd fallen in love with her. Rein looked up, aware that Wyatt stared at him in disbelief.

"I'll be damned," Wyatt said. "You're in love with her, aren't you?"

 files

She stood at the back door and stared up at the black velvet sky awash with stars. She knew what she must do and that Rein would think the worst of her. But what choice did she have? How many times in the past few weeks had she gazed up at the sparkling night sky, amazed by her fortune to have found this place? If such beauty could exist, surely it was by design and not merely by coincidence. That realization gave her a glimmer of hope. Hope that Providence had finally smiled down on her, given her the family she'd always dreamt of, given her security, purpose, and yes, someone to love. *Love.*

She'd been infatuated with Rein Mackenzie from the first time she laid eyes on him. And though he didn't feel the same, she didn't regret one moment they had together. When she realized her feelings ran deeper, she hoped that he'd discover something worth fighting to keep. Unfortunately, he hadn't. Instead, he confronted her with the truth and ended whatever it was they had. Maybe she'd been a fool to think that working together, sharing similar ideas, and working on the cabins during the day, then going to his bed at night would evolve into something more.

The truth was, he'd been honest with her from the start, making it clear that she didn't really belong here. But she'd let that earlier trait go by the wayside and hadn't been honest with herself, allowing his perfect body to dominate her thoughts night and day. She'd crossed the line and now she'd pay the price.

She swallowed the lump in her throat and stuffed what few belongings she had in her duffle. Without a backward glance, she stepped out into the pitch-black night. A cool breeze touched her face, cooling the brief tears she'd cried as she packed. Her boots crunched the gravel beneath her feet as she walked up the lane, past the barn. For a moment, her gaze settled on the main house, where most of the windows were dark now. Inside, Wyatt, Aimee, and Dalton slept. They were a family—along with Rein and Michael Greyfeather and his kin. She pressed her lips together, holding back an onslaught of sadness. She'd never truly fit in.

She wondered if Wyatt's warning to Rein had been out of concern for the two of them, or simply watching over Rein's reputation regarding the future of the cabin project. After all, what would happen if word got out that the tawdry Vegas half-sister had slept around with Jed's nephew? An owl hooted in one of the tall pines near the house, and she stumbled, catching her bag and clutching her heart at the same time. The array of wildlife wasn't something she'd miss, but there was much that she would. It would take time to bounce back from this change, but she knew it was best for everyone that she go.

"Leaving without saying goodbye?"

A gasp tore from her throat and she whirled on her heel to face Rein. He emerged from the shadows of his workshop, wiping his hands on his jeans. As he stepped beneath the yard light, his features seemed sharper, focused. "It's a long walk to town."

"I didn't think anyone else was awake."

"Clearly. Guess that saves time on messy goodbyes?"

Her spine stiffened. Some nerve this cowboy had. He'd been the one to end things and in truth she should be grateful. While she had planned to leave to protect her family, he'd simply given her the green light not to tarry. "The cabins are nearly done, Aimee's ready for the baby, and I have a plan to go back to school. I only said that I'd stay until the time came to move on." She shrugged. "It's time."

"And what about us?" he asked taking a step closer. She could see the fire in his blue eyes and frankly, it puzzled her. She backed up until she smacked into the tailgate of Dalton's truck.

"We're over. You made that perfectly clear."

He crossed his arms and regarded her. "How'd you plan to leave?" He sidestepped her comment.

"The main road's not that far." She volleyed. "Once there, I figure a friendly trucker will come along sooner or later."

"Right. And in the meantime, how did you plan to stave off a wolf or bobcat?"

She hadn't thought of that. "I have pepper spray...if necessary. Besides, Michael says that most wildlife is more afraid of us."

"Tell that to a hungry mountain lion."

She sighed and adjusted the bag over her shoulder. "Well, I'm leaving and if you're that worried about it, you could offer to take me to Billings."

"Does this have anything to do with the phone call you received earlier today?"

The less he knew the better off they'd all be. It had been almost two hours since she'd given Angelo her flight information. He'd be expecting her soon, telling her again what a bright girl she was in doing what's best. Yes, best for him, best for Elaina, and more importantly, best for her newfound family. But "best" for her? Hardly, but she had little choice until she could meet Angelo face-to-face. "It's none of your concern, Rein." She shifted the bag and turned to leave, jerked back when he grabbed it from her. She stumbled, righting herself and then faced him. Fury seethed through her. "What the hell do you want from me?"

Rein held her bag captive. "Let's start with the truth. Why are you sneaking off in the middle of the night?"

Despite her desire to keep her emotions in check, her eyes pooled. *Damn him.* She blinked away the tears. "Okay, you're right. I didn't want any messy goodbyes." She reached for her duffle and he yanked it out of reach. "Are you enjoying this? You were right. Isn't that what you wanted to hear?"

He shook his head. "No, Liberty. I want the truth. This isn't about me ending things between us, or that the cabins are done. It's not even about you wanting to move on. There is something else and we can stand here until sunrise, but I swear I'm going to get it out of you."

She planted her fists on her hips and stared at him. "It's my life. I can handle it."

"What aren't you telling me?" He continued to prod her, though for the love of all that's holy, she couldn't understand why.

"Look, when we started this," she waved her hand in the air, "this, whatever we had, we both agreed not to discuss our past or the future. It was fun. I had a blast. Now give me the damn duffle bag." An errant tear escaped and she swiped it from her cheek in haste.

He hesitated as though debating whether to relinquish her bag. "And this is what you want—to just leave?"

She released a weary sigh and nodded. Hopefully, he was

done asking questions. "Yes, I do. I think it's best for everyone...if I leave." She held her hand out waiting for him to hand over the duffle.

"What about you? What's best for you? Going back to the life you had? The one that you risked everything in order to seek out the half-brothers you hardly knew?" He shook his head. "You're running scared, Liberty. Maybe it's time you stopped trying to handle things alone and trust your family."

"Family or you? Because from the first day you've made it clear that I don't belong here."

He at least had the decency to look at the ground. She'd nailed him to the tree.

"Guilty." He raised his eyes to hers. "I admit being hard on you at first. I carried around some prejudices that I didn't realize were there and I'm sorry about that. I was wrong. I'd never met anyone like you before, Liberty."

She offered a quick laugh. "Until you wound up in my bed. Amazing how fast perspectives can change, right? Well at least you got the curiosity out of your system." She saw the flash of hurt in his eyes, but she wouldn't knuckle under. He'd gotten what he wanted hadn't he?

"Stop it." He demanded and took another step toward her.

"Aw come on, Rein. Admit, you were curious. I'm an unusual distraction. Look at me. I'm nothing at all like Aimee or...Sally. *That's* the kind of woman a man like you is looking for. The kind that will settle down. Be happy to have the white picket fence and a fairytale ending."

"That doesn't speak highly of Aimee, or Sally, but I'll let it go because you're upset. And for the record, how the hell do you know what I need?" He dropped the bag to the ground with a thud and closed the gap between them.

"Because I know your type. You, Wyatt and Dalton—you'd sacrifice anything for the woman you love. You're just built that way." She closed her eyes and turned her face from his piercing look. She couldn't look at him in the eye. She didn't want him to see her vulnerability. She didn't want him to see that she wanted to be the woman he'd sacrifice anything for.

He brushed her cheek with his knuckles. "Maybe you're exactly the type of woman I need, Liberty. Have you given any thought to that?" His fingers lifted her chin, turning her gaze to his.

She blinked away new tears. "Please don't do this." Her warning lacked any punch. She couldn't take much more. Especially since she'd convinced herself she had nothing left for her here at End of the Line. Her chin quivered.

"Don't leave us, Liberty. Aimee's going to need you after the baby comes. Wyatt and Dalton haven't had near enough time yet to get to know you. You haven't even experienced a Montana Christmas yet." He softly touched her bottom lip with the pad of his thumb, sending a familiar tingle up her spine.

"And what about you, Rein? You haven't said why you don't want me to leave."

He searched her eyes. "I'd miss you, Liberty. I know what I want, and god-love them, it's not anyone like Aimee or Sally. But there's a lot to consider, Liberty. For starters, our difference in age. There are more than a few years between us. I'm settled here. This is my life. You're just starting out, trying to find your place, what you want in your life. I can't, no, I won't ask you to give that up, just so you'll stay here with me."

"You're going to have to give me a better reason than that, Rein."

He released a sigh. "Because if I do, I won't know if you stayed because you wanted to or because you thought you might just give this a test run and then leave."

"You really think I'm that flighty?"

His lips curved into a smile. "Darlin', you're taking off in the middle of the night."

She placed her hand over his. "I didn't think you'd care. We had an agreement. I tried to hold that up."

He took her face in his hands. "To hell with the agreement. The truth is I thought I'd be able to keep you and my emotions at arm's length. But I fell in love with you and the thought scares the hell out of me."

"Why? Because you think that I'll drag you along like Caroline did, then drop you for something better? I may be younger than you, Rein Mackenzie, but I'm not stupid." She leaned forward and placed a chaste kiss on his mouth. "I'm just glad that Caroline's not only a snob, but stupid."

He brought his mouth to hers igniting the need in her as always. Catching her breath, she studied his fiery blue eyes and for the first time, saw her future. But if they were to have a future, she could no longer keep any secrets from him. She had to tell him about Angelo. Unfortunately, his mouth trailing kisses down her throat and his fingers busy with the buttons of her blouse distracted her. She wanted him with a reckless need. It was always that way between them. "Rein," she spoke his name with a sigh as he caressed her, causing her mind to spin.

"Tell me I'm not imagining this, Liberty. Tell me that you feel the same."

The cool metal of the truck pressed against the thin cotton of her shirt. He lowered his mouth to hers in a series of hot, relentless kisses. She could barely think, she didn't want to. She wanted him, all of him. His was the face she wanted to wake up next to every day. "I do feel the same, but there's something I need to tell you...it's about my past."

His hands dropped to her waist and leaned his forehead to hers. She heard his ragged breathing. "I want to strip off these clothes and make love to you right over there, under that tree with the moonlight shining down on your beautiful face." He sighed heavily as he carefully refastened her blouse. "But we need to talk, you're right." He cupped her face and smiled. "But don't think that this isn't taking every ounce of willpower to achieve this." He touched his lips to hers and groaned.

A bright light severed the kiss and Liberty had to blink a couple of times and shade her eyes.

Dalton hurried toward them. Wyatt close behind. "Rein?

Thank God you're still awake." He flashed the beam toward Liberty, then back to Rein.

"God bless it, Dalton, Can you shine that damn thing elsewhere?"

"Sorry. Rebecca just called. They've taken Michael to the Billings ER. She thinks it's a heart attack."

"Jesus," Rein muttered. His eyes darted to Liberty.

"You go. We can talk when you get back."

"You won't leave." Wyatt trotted toward them, his hand came down on Liberty's shoulder. Dalton was already in the truck. "I need a favor, Liberty. Aimee's too tired to make the trip. I let her sleep. Can you stay with her?"

She nodded, relieved that it appeared no one else had seen her duffle bag and started asking a bunch of questions.

"You coming, Rein?" Dalton shouted from the cab.

"Go." She placed a quick kiss on his mouth. "I'll be here."

ख

Rein hated hospitals. They conjured up ghosts in his past, unpleasant ghosts of memories that up to now he'd kept tucked away in a dark corner of this mind. He tossed his empty coffee cup in the trash and glanced at Rebecca seated with Betty in the Emergency waiting room. More than an hour had passed since they arrived. It'd taken Betty less than twenty minutes to show up for one of her oldest friends. She'd made a beeline for the older woman, who in Rein's eyes, had never looked as weary as she did at this moment. Rebecca had always appeared calm, strong in the face of adversity.

"Have you called the girls?" Betty asked. Rebecca nodded and collapsed into the purple and gray waiting chair. The hospital had touted the recent makeover provided for by private donations. The colors were result of a study done that showed that they could provide greater calm to those in traumatic situations. Rebecca sniffed and looked up at Betty, her eyes filled with concern.

"I can't stand this." Clearly, the color scheme hadn't worked on his brother, Dalton. "I'm going to go see if I can find someone who knows what the hell's going on."

Rein knelt in front of Rebecca. "Can I get you anything? A cup of coffee, tea?"

"Tea would be nice, Rein. Thank you." Her voice remained steady.

He nodded. "Comin' up." Next to Jed and his brothers, she and Michael were like family.

Betty, silent now with her head bowed, hands clasped, chatted with God. She was one of those few and rare women that lived her religion. Not in terms of attending Sunday services every week, as they were open for the Sunday Brunch Buffet. But she believed in a higher being and Rein wasn't about to interrupt her thoughts. He brought Rebecca's tea, holding her hands in his as she took the cup. "He's going to be fine."

She nodded. Her soft brown eyes looked up at him. "He has much to live for. Our lovely Angelique is back home. It is good for Emily to be with her mother again."

Rein had heard Michael talking once to Wyatt about Angelique's time in the rehab center. She'd entered the facility on her own after a long bout with alcoholism and the accident that claimed her husband's life and nearly hers and Emily's. Emily had only been two at the time and given over to the care of her only surviving kin, Michael and Rebecca. It had been a long road, first recovering from her injuries and then her rehabilitation. Because Aimee had wanted Emily to be their flower girl, Aimee and Sally together agreed it only right to include Angelique in the bridal party. Rein nodded and realized the woman's mind must be filled with many memories. He understood that all too well. He patted her hand. "It's going to be okay, you'll see."

Needing a breath of fresh air, Rein walked into the hallway to look for either of his brothers. Given the hour, he was surprised at the traffic in the ER. A set of worried parents with a sick child stood at the admissions desk. Another doctor rushed past him and through a set of swinging doors that led to the operating room. However, he didn't see Wyatt or Dalton.

Taking a quick look into the waiting room, he signaled to Betty that he was stepping outside. The double doors whooshed open and Rein took a deep breath, grateful for the cool air.

"I hate hospitals."

He recognized the voice and looked in the shadows to see Wyatt seated on one of the concrete benches near the side of the building. "Yeah, me, too."

Neither man seemed to know what to say next. Wyatt spoke first, "You know Aimee's talked about having the baby at home, with a midwife. Did you know that Rebecca is a certified midwife?" He shook his head and clasped his hands over his knees. "I don't know. The idea in theory sounds appealing, but what if something happened?" He glanced at Rein. "Any word yet?"

He shook his head. "Not yet. Dalton went to try to find someone. There's an awful lot going on here tonight. I wonder if it's always this crazy. That could be why it seems things are taking a little longer."

Wyatt nodded, removed his hat and raked his hand through his dark, brown hair. Rein noticed the small shock of silver at Wyatt's temples. "You know what they say...when one person dies, another is born." He looked up at Rein. "Michael's been like a father to us all."

"And he's a tough old Indian. Besides, he's got Betty in there talking to the Man upstairs."

Wyatt chuckled, and then pulled out his phone. "It's almost two a.m. You suppose Aimee's doing okay? I hate to call and wake them. She didn't feel well after supper. Her stomach felt queasy. Is that normal?"

Rein rubbed his eyes. "I've never heard you fuss this much

over anything in your life, Wyatt. Remember this is the woman that managed to keep a car full of kids safe when it nearly went over a cliff last winter. "It'd had been a December to remember, for certain and most of it had happened while Rein and Dalton were stuck in Iowa during an unexpected early season storm that obliterated travel the three days before Christmas. The event that started with Aimee bringing out her kids for a pre-holiday field trip, turned out to be a pivotal, life-changing moment in his older brother's life and as time went on, in Aimee's life as well.

Wyatt nodded. "I know, you're right. She's a strong woman. It's just that sometimes she looks so damn uncomfortable and I feel I feel guilty about that. I wish I could make things easier for her."

"Yeah, well, she played a part in this too. She's going to be fine. And Wyatt, you're going to make one hell of a dad."

"Yeah? You think I can do it?"

"I know so. Look how you handled all those kids in the house."

"I had Aimee's guidance. She's amazing with those kids."

"My point exactly. Besides, if anything had changed, we'd have heard from Liberty."

"Yeah, I suppose that's true."

The ER doors swooshed open and Dalton appeared. "Doc's in the waiting room talking to Rebecca."

They followed him, crowding as best they could into the small room.

"We've gotten the preliminary tests back and they confirm what we suspected. Your husband has suffered a heart attack. However, we won't know the severity of the episode until we do what is called a catheterization to determine the extent of the blockage in the arteries." The doctor held Rebecca's hand. "We'll need you to sign a few permission forms stating your wish for us to proceed. As with any surgery there is always a measure of risk, however, from what I've seen thus far, and if my suspicions prove true, we can get things taken care of relatively quickly and have him back on his feet in no time."

Rebecca waited patiently as the doctor finished. "If you feel this is what needs to be done, then yes, I will sign the papers." She followed the doctor from the room. Rein and his brothers trailed dutifully behind.

The doctor glanced over his shoulder. "Are these your sons?"

"Not by blood, but in every other sense, yes."

Rein placed his arm around the tiny woman and kissed her temple. He looked at his brothers and nodded toward the waiting room. "Well go wait with Betty, unless you need one of us to go with you?"

Rebecca touched his cheek and smiled. "Thank you, I can manage. I won't be long."

CR

Rein awoke with a start and a crick in his neck. He rolled his head side to side, for a moment trying to remember where he was and why. He'd dozed off and fallen into a deep sleep. When his vision cleared, he realized a beautiful dark-eyed woman sat across from him. She caught his eye and smiled.

"Hello, Rein." Her coal-black hair, sleek and beautiful like her Aunt Rebecca's, she had pulled over one shoulder in a loose braid. The buff colored suede jacket she wore, her denim jeans and worn cowboy boots reminded him of how pretty she'd always been, even back in middle school.

"I must have dozed off." He sat up and rubbed his eyes, then looked around. Wyatt and Dalton too, were fast asleep, one seated upright with his hat pulled over his eyes, and the other sprawled out on the small loveseat couch.

"You were all asleep when we got back to the room. Aunt Rebecca just fell asleep. Poor thing. This has been hard on her." She motioned toward the coffee station, and using her coat as a pillow, eased her aunt to the small couch and covered her with a blue blanket the nurse had brought in.

Rein checked his watch, Three-thirty. Surely, they'd finished the catheterization by now. "Has anyone been in to talk to you?" he whispered as he followed Angelique around the small countertop.

"They came in about thirty minutes ago and said they found the blockage and did the angioplasty. They were preparing to put in a stint to keep the artery open. There's only one surgeon and they said it's been an unusually busy tonight."

"Must be the full moon," Rein chuckled.

"Now you sound like my uncle." She smiled and poured a cup of coffee. She offered it to him and though it smelled freshly brewed, he declined.

"I've had enough, and clearly it's not helping." His back teeth were practically floating, truth be told. "I'm going to find a restroom and splash some cold water on my face. We should be hearing something soon."

"How long have you been here?" Her gaze bounced to Dalton and back again. Rein knew from Sally that Angelique had had a crush on Dalton at one time, but he'd turned a blind eye, too much of a ladies man to notice the quiet young woman.

"Not long after they brought him in." He held her eyes a moment and she quickly saw his curiosity.

"I got Aunt Rebecca's phone call, of course, but I had to finish my shift at the market."

"You're working two jobs?" Rein noticed then the dark circles, touched up by makeup beneath her beautiful eyes.

"It's just until I can get back on my feet. I have some obligations I want to get rid of."

His mind wandered back to the ranch, wondering how Liberty and Aimee were doing. He thought of the kiss he'd shared with Liberty and wondered what had prompted her to leave in the middle of the night. Thank God he'd found her before she left, so he could tell her how he felt.

"Rein?"

"Uh, sorry, yeah."

"I asked how Aimee and Liberty are doing. I haven't seen them since the wedding."

"Great, they're doing great." Despite the fact that Liberty had nearly flown the coop without saying goodbye. "Aimee is getting big, I mean big. I still have to wonder if she isn't carrying two."

"They've done an ultra-sound, haven't they?"

Rein nodded. "Yep, and they say it's just one, but I have my doubts."

"My aunt mentioned your cabin project. How's that coming?"

"Very well, thanks. We've been working hard on them since the wedding. Hoping to open up next spring, if possible. Maybe it will generate a little business for the town as well. Wyatt thinks we maybe ought to open it up to small groups, like summer camp for inner city kids."

"Wyatt Kinnison wants to have kids out to the ranch? I heard he used to be quite a hermit—Grinch, I believe, was the term my aunt used."

"Yeah, "Rein laughed quietly. "People do change." He thought about how much he'd changed being around Liberty the past few weeks. Even now, the thought made his heart twitch. They weren't ready to walk down the aisle by any means. They had a lot to talk about, a lot more to find out about each other. In the last few hours, he'd come to realize that he felt they were just beginning something good, and not ending it.

Angelique took a sip from the cup and once again her eyes darted a look at Dalton.

"Then again, there is something to be said for consistency." Rein smiled.

She raised her brow. "He's pretty much the same guy I remember in school." Her tone was matter-of-fact, the sound of a woman maybe hardened around the edges from life. Still, he detected softness when she looked at Dalton and while he loved his brother dearly, there were things about him that didn't make him commitment material. Before he opened his mouth and said something he might regret, Rein excused himself in search of the restroom.

Another hour passed before a nurse came in and told Rebecca and Angelique they could go in for a few minutes to see Michael. He'd be in ICU until they felt ready to transfer him, perhaps tomorrow, to a regular room.

Rein sat with his brothers, staring at his phone, thinking about Liberty, where things might be headed between them. He wondered how Wyatt and Dalton would take to the idea.

"Did you get any sleep?" Dalton asked as he stretched his arms over his head. He tilted his head back and forth and released a massive yawn.

"A little. I had a nice chat with Angelique." Rein waited, gauging his brother's reaction. "She looks good. She was always pretty, you know in school, but she's grown up to be a beautiful woman." Rein met Dalton's bleary gaze. "I heard she had quite a crush on you."

Dalton chuckled and offered a wicked grin. "One of many. What can I say?"

"You ever take her out?"

"Like a date? No," he scoffed.

He shot back his answer so quick, it made Rein curious. "Really? Someone as pretty as—"

"Leave it alone."

Rein's phone buzzed, and Dalton's, then Wyatt's phone's followed. All three were part of End of the Line's volunteer firefighting squad. Though they were called primarily as back up in extreme cases such as brush fires.

"Jesus," Rein muttered. His concerned gaze met Wyatt's. "It's the ranch."

Chapter Ten

*L*iberty awoke coughing, her thoughts disoriented. She stumbled her way across the hall following Aimee's cries for help. A thick, heavy haze of wood smoke permeated the air. Her mind scrambled trying to remember what she'd done before she lay down to rest for a few minutes on Rein's bed. One by one, she heard the alarms going off throughout the rest of the house.

She rushed into the bathroom, soaked a towel and placing it over her mouth, made her way back in the hall. Aimee, holding her round belly, stumbled from her bedroom, falling into Liberty's grasp. "Breathe in this. We've got to get out of here." She placed the towel over Aimee's mouth. She had no idea what started the blaze, but a house made of logs wouldn't last long. With a solid grasp on Aimee's arm, she moved toward the front room. Smoke billowed from the kitchen door.

She looked up in time to see a dark figure move across the back deck and at that instant knew this was no accident. She'd not shown up at the airport and this was Angelo's retaliation, his promise to make things worse. Whether Franco realized anyone was home didn't matter. His chief concern included making sure Liberty didn't live, and it didn't matter who got in the way. That meant Aimee and the baby were in as much

159

danger. But Liberty would die before she let any harm come to them. "We need to get outside. Come on. Through Rein's room. The side porch." She shoved Aimee through the room.

The roar of the fire on the roof grew to a deafening decibel. The heat became worse, tugging at her lungs, sucking the air from them.

Her heart ached for all the memories that would be lost—the nursery, the pictures, Rein's beautifully crafted furniture, priceless mementos turned to ash and all because of her. She refocused her efforts to get Aimee to safety before Franco could see them. Slipping out the side door, she helped Aimee over the railing and kept low as she crept to the safety behind the pile of timber at the side of the house. She prayed that her nine-one-one call would get a fire truck here in time to save the buildings near the house. Her eyes burned. She squinted in the dim light and though dark, the flames shooting from the roof now illuminated a large portion of the yard. Liberty eased the cloth away from Aimee's face. Tears streamed down her friend's face. Her blonde hair was streaked with soot. "Breath slow, are you okay?"

Aimee nodded and proceeded to throw up in the grass. Liberty held her shoulders, keeping an eye out for Franco. She swallowed as gasp as he appeared at the front of the house, not more than a few hundred yards from where they hid. He looked up at his handiwork, his grin the epitome of evil, glowing in the fire's light.

"You stay here," Liberty whispered to Aimee. "Promise me."

The terrified woman grabbed her arm. "No, you stay here with me. Help will be here soon."

"I'm going to lure him away from the house. Wyatt's truck is out front. When you see your chance, you get over there and hightail it to town."

Aimee searched her eyes. "I'm not leaving you here."

"Aimee, you have to think of your baby, Wyatt's baby." She glanced over her shoulder at the house. Glass shattered and she heard a whoop of delight from Franco. The idiot had no idea that the fire had been reported. He was too full of himself to realize anyone had been home. Either that, or he figured those inside had already succumbed to the smoke. "I know this guy, Aimee. This is my fault." She choked back a sob and cupped her sister-in-law's face. "Do as I say. You remember where Wyatt keeps his spare key?"

"We should wait together."

Liberty peered through a slit between the logs. Franco had his phone to his ear, no doubt giving Angelo the news that he'd done his duty. "Do as I say, Aimee. Wait until I get his attention. Then run and don't look back."

"No, Liberty, don't." She tightened her grip. Liberty patted her friend's hand and remembered how she'd been the first one to make her feel welcome.

"I was a fast runner in school. Don't worry." She didn't need to stay another moment to know that Aimee would continue to fight the idea. But at the moment, she had little choice. She had to get Franco away from that truck and give Aimee the time she needed to escape.

Careful not to make a sound, she snuck behind Rein's woodworking shop and ran out into the lane that led to the barn and the cabins. 'You plan on leaving without me, Franco?" She yelled above the din. The smoke in her lungs stifled her voice and she began to choke, coughing up soot and slime from her throat. He spotted her and as she hoped, took off after her. Her lungs felt like lead as she stumbled down the dirt lane. Hours before, she'd planned on leaving the ranch. Rein had stopped her with his poetic confession of needing her, wanting her to stay. It seemed ironic that she might now die in the exact spot where she'd had her first glimpse at her future. The horses, housed inside the barn, sensed the danger, and whinnied restlessly in their stalls. She snuck in through the back of the barn and one by one opened the stalls, swatting at the horses, getting them out of the building in case a spark should send the building into flames. She froze as she spotted

Franco's silhouette standing at the opposite entrance, unfazed by the stampede.

"None of this would have happened if you'd just come home like Angelo wanted."

She stayed in the shadows and searched for something, anything that she could defend against his attack.

"Game over, sweetheart. You know we can't have any witnesses. He ordered this after he hung up. He figured you'd go to the police and you'd mess things up. So, he left it to me. And you know I am a professional."

Liberty grabbed a shovel and pressed her shoulder against the back door of the barn, anticipating that he'd follow. When he didn't immediately burst through the door, she crept to the corner of the barn and peered around the edge. Like heaven to her ears, the sound of the fire truck blaring its horn sounded over the roar of the house now almost entirely engulfed in flames. Blue and red lights flashed eerily over the landscape. Close behind Dalton's truck followed, barreling at full speed, its headlights bouncing over the ruts in the gravel road.

Startled by the onslaught of people barring his escape, Franco faced the entourage, his body silhouetted by the bright lights. Liberty, seizing her chance, ran up behind him, the shovel poised over her head. At that instant, Dalton's truck made a sharp turn, and crashed through the split rail fence that edged the dirt lane. Blinded by the light, Liberty held her position, squinting for better aim at Franco while distracted. She swung the shovel at his head with the purpose of a baseball player, barely aware of Rein shouting as he leaped from the truck.

"Hold it right there, don't move." He ran toward them, even before the truck had fully stopped.

The shovel connected to Franco's shoulder and the jarring impact of it sent tingles shooting through her arms. To her surprise, a loud explosion followed and a flare of light streamed through the air. She watched in shock as Franco crumpled at her feet.

"Liberty?" Rein's voice sounded puzzled.

She dropped the shovel and ran toward him as he dropped to his knees in front of her.

"What is it? What's—" Her eyes widened. She couldn't breathe. She stared at the dark stain beginning to soak through his grey tee shirt.

"I think I've been shot."

Epilogue

"*W*yatt looks like he's been dragged through a knot-hole backward." Betty shook her head. "This is the second time in twenty-four hours that I've found myself in this waiting room. And folks say nothing exciting ever happens in small towns. Come here, darlin'. You must be half out of your mind."

Liberty walked into the big woman's embrace, welcoming the warmth of her hug. Tears pricked at the back of her eyes. It'd been several hours since they'd arrived back at the hospital. They'd rushed Rein into surgery with a bullet wound to the shoulder and hurried Aimee to the floor to have her and the baby checked over.

"We all pretty much look like shit," Dalton mumbled and downed his third cup of coffee since sunrise. He looked at Liberty, removed his ball cap, and pushed a hand through his thick black curls. "Doc says Aimee and the baby are going to be fine. You did the right thing getting her out of there when you did."

Tears pooled in Liberty's eyes as she stepped from Betty's arms. She felt nothing like the heroine they'd painted her to be. "But the ranch. You're beautiful home that Jed built."

Wyatt stood then and met her in the middle of the room. He took her hand and pulled her close, hugging her tight.

"The house can be rebuilt and thanks to your techno-geek

brother over there," he nodded toward Dalton who raised a weary hand. "All of our important documents are safely tucked away in a deposit box at the bank. He's even got all of our pictures on a flash drive."

"You can thank me later."

Wyatt chuckled, gave her another squeeze and kissed the top of her head. "You did good, baby sister."

"If I'd not come. If I'd just gone back like Angelo wanted, none of this would have happened."

He held her at arm's length, regarding her with a curious smile. "You're right, I suppose. But Aimee wouldn't have known her brave, wonderful sister-in-law. Our baby wouldn't have an aunt to teach him how to be ornery and, we'd have never known we had such a courageous sister." He narrowed his gaze. "And Rein, well...."

She covered her face, reliving the moment when she realized he'd been shot. "Oh God, when I saw he'd been shot, that I'd been the one to cause the gun to misfire...."

"That sequence of events may well have saved his life, Liberty. He's a tough old cuss. He'll be fine. The idiot leapt out of the truck before we could stop. Hell, that alone could have killed him. Guess he had more important things on his mind."

Liberty sniffed and met her brother's dark, gentle eyes. For the first time, she felt a sense of belonging, the warmth of family.

"You know he's going to need someone with a keen sense of design to help him rebuild the house."

"What if he doesn't want to see me?"

Dalton's arm dropped over her shoulder. "I'd be happy to knock some sense into his head if you like. Seems to me that you two have been dancing around each other long enough, don't you think?"

Her cheeks warmed under the twin scrutiny of her brothers. They seemed to have more faith in Rein's forgiveness than she did. Guess she needed to find out for herself. She straightened and quickly swiped her fingers over her cheeks.

"How do I look?"

They glanced at each other, then her. "Like hell," they answered together.

Betty's laughter peeled through the waiting room. Liberty stepped into her brother's embrace. It felt good to belong.

Nerves gnawed at her gut, Liberty peeked into the room and met the nurse as she finished her hourly assessment. "Just a few minutes. He's still weak from surgery."

She pressed her lips together and held back the tears that threatened to escape as she stepped cautiously into the dark room. The dim light behind his bed cast him in a surreal blue-white glow. He lay with his eyes closed. She stood staring down at his ruggedly handsome, face. Even without benefit of a razor he was beautiful. His upper body, bare except for the gauze bandages wrapped around his rib cage and shoulder, showed a stark contrast to his bronzed skin. Many times she'd watched him sleep after they'd made love, and she cautioned herself not to get too close, not to lose her heart. But she had, and she couldn't turn back now, even if she tried. Her gaze traveled across the wires and tubes connecting him to various machines and came to rest on the steady blip of his heart on the monitor. How many times had she fallen asleep listening to that strong, steady beat?

"Hey," his husky voice startled her. He pried open one eye and then the other and offered her a sloppy grin.

She walked around to his side, and bit down on her lip determined not to cry.

"Aw Libby. Don't, baby."

"I'm so, so sorry. I didn't know he had a gun."

He took her hand and threaded his fingers through hers. "Careful there, slick. You know what happens when you try to apologize." He used her words and offered a weak grin.

"You might have been killed."

"Hey." He coughed and then winced at the pain. "The way I figure it, he might have had better aim had it not been for that hit with the shovel, slugger." He licked his lips and glanced at the water glass. "I could use a little help."

He took a sip through a straw and settled back on the pillow, releasing a deep sigh. "How are Aimee and the baby?"

He held tight to her hand, not letting go.

"The doctor says they'll both be fine. He wants to keep her here overnight, as a precaution."

"Any word on Michael?"

In all the chaos of the past few hours, she'd nearly forgotten her brief conversation with Rebecca. "Doing very well, I guess. They told Rebecca she could take him home in a day or two. He'll come back in a week or so to start rehab and go over his diet."

"No more taste-testing Rebecca's pies." He smiled and she noticed the fine smile lines creasing the corners of his eyes. A gorgeous cowboy with laugh lines? She could do a helluva lot worse, and truth be told, she'd had her fill of losers in her life. She glanced at their hands, seeing that he hadn't let go and decided maybe she should stop running, that maybe what she'd been looking for was right in front of her. But could he still want her after all that had happened? Right now, doped up on pain meds, groggy still from surgery, he'd likely just glad to be alive—and God, so was she.

"What about that Franco guy? What happened to him?"

"Besides a very bad headache?"

"That's my slugger."

"His name is Franco Martinez. One of Angelo's goons."

"You make it sound like the mafia."

"Angelo is bad news. It's one of the main reasons I left like I did. I'd hoped he'd forget about me, find another girl to charm. I hadn't counted on his pride or his greed to want revenge."

"Revenge? For what?'

Liberty sighed and pulled a chair close to the bed. Rein resumed holding her hand. "He talked me into dancing at one of his clubs. He bought me things, an apartment, clothes, but I began to realize there were strings attached to his affections.

And as I began to pull away, he became more possessive. There was talk that he used the club for drug trafficking. That's when I decided I needed to get out."

"Smart girl."

She shrugged. "Except that he found me and tried to hurt my family by sending Franco who I'm guessing has a list of arsons under his belt. I saw his face as he stared at the fire. I couldn't believe he could do something so horrific, worse, because of me."

"Liberty, this wasn't your fault. It's because Angelo is a very dangerous and sick man. I just want to make sure he can't hurt you ever again."

She proceeded to tell him how her friend Elaina had escaped after Angelo left her with one of his guards and managed to get to a neighbors to call the police. "I owe Elaina so much for what she's done for me," Liberty said. "She and I, and a few others at the club have agreed to testify against Angelo and some of the shady dealings they've seen go down at the club."

"And what about this Franco?" Rein asked.

"I think Franco will be only too happy to strike a deal with authorities, once he realizes that they've closed the club and taken Angelo into custody on some other charges while they do their investigation."

"Did Angelo ever threaten you personally?" Rein's brow furrowed.

"By phone, yes. It became his habit to threaten anyone who didn't do as he said. He enjoys controlling people, just like my father."

"You don't have to go back. You have a home and a family here, now."

She searched his eyes. "I may have to go back to testify."

"And I'll be right there with you. I imagine, so will Wyatt and Dalton."

A lump formed in her throat. She held his gaze. "How'd I get so lucky to find you?"

He motioned his head for her to come closer. She scooted nearer the bedside.

"Closer, up here."

She stood and leaned over him, careful not to touch him, though she wanted to more than anything. His blue eyes darkened and she grinned. "Those meds must be working great."

He took her chin in his fingertips and drew her face to his, searching her eyes.

"*You* are what's good for me, Miss Liberty Belle." He pulled her face down, touching his mouth to hers in a soft, lingering kiss.

"You realize I'm going to need someone really good to help me design and rebuild the house."

Her heart sank as she thought once more of the beautiful home they'd lost. She couldn't look him in his eyes. Liberty shook her head, unable to stop the tears that had built inside her. He slid his hand around her neck and pulled her to him, tenderly kissing her forehead.

"It was time to get new furniture anyway."

Liberty choked out a short laugh. "It makes me sick."

"I'm grateful you're quick thinking saved as much of the ranch as it did. Things could have been much worse, Liberty. Much worse."

She blinked and cleared her focus. "I suppose."

"So, about that help?"

She smiled through her tears. "Wyatt suggested you might need some help."

"I've always admired his older brother wisdom. Besides, you can't leave me to do this with Dalton. I'm liable to kill him."

She snuggled close to his side, her face inches from his. "I am pretty good at what I do, I have to admit."

"In more ways than one." His husky response sent a delicious shiver through her. She kissed him, savoring the taste of his mouth still cool from the ice water.

"Hmm, I like that." He looked at her with a curious sparkle in his eye. "After we finish with that, I'm hoping you might help me with another project."

"What's that? More cabins?" She pressed his palm against her cheek, grateful he was okay, grateful for so many things.

"I have plans for this house I want to build on the lake. It's close enough to the main ranch, but far enough away from privacy. Always thought it'd be a good place to start a family."

Her eyes welled. "You have anyone in mind, slick?"

His blue eyes sparkled as he spoke. "Well, whoever it is would have to have a high tolerance for family dinners, holidays, and more chaos than you can imagine. Thought maybe you might be interested."

Liberty's eyes watered. She thought of all they'd been through in such a short time, of all that lay ahead. She'd never met a man like him, someone she could work beside each day, and make love to each night. It sounded like big sky heaven to her. "I have to warn you, I've got so many ideas buzzing around in my head with what we can accomplish together, it's liable to take a lifetime to achieve them all."

"Does it involve those furry handcuffs?"

She grinned. "It might." No more running. No more looking over her shoulder. She belonged here and somehow she had a feeling that Jed and Eloise had reconciled, and maybe they were smiling down on their legacy right now.

"I like the way you think." He kissed her and a new beginning, a new world opened in her heart.

Dear Readers,

I hope you enjoyed Rein and Liberty's story in RUSTLER'S HEART. If you'd like to read Wyatt and Aimee's story, you can read it in Rugged Hearts, in both print and e-book formats. Coming up next is the tale of the stubborn and wild, Dalton Kinnison and Angelique; a hometown girl who has harbored a secret crush on the least tamable Kinnison male since high school. Personal tragedy brings her back to End of the Line, with the secrets and gossip that goes along with a small town. But a misstep on Dalton's part will be the pivotal point in the ranch's future and only one woman can save him—Angelique.

Watch for RENEGADE HEART, next in the Kinnison Legacy series. Meantime, enjoy a sample chapter of the first book in the Kinnison Legacy series, RUGGED HEARTS.

~Amanda

If Rustler's Heart should become a good choice for your book club, I've added a few questions here that might help with a discussion:

Rein has an idyllic view of the dream that his Uncle Jed describes in his journal. It's taken him a long time to convince his brothers, especially Wyatt to invest in the "cabin" project. In theory, the concept seems altruistic and Rein believes that accepting Liberty's request for temporary shelter may be the very thing that's needed to convince Wyatt of the worthiness of the project. Have you ever been in a position where you needed to be the example in order to convince someone that a project or person is worthy of a chance? Like Rein, was your "looks *good on paper,* theory challenged when faced with reality? How did you handle it?

Rein's former girlfriend shows up and it seems like she's interested in Rein, but for what purpose? Could it have been her curiosity to see if Rein was still interested in her or do you think she came to rub his nose in her success? What did you think of what she said about Liberty? Did Rein handle that situation the way you might have? Should Caroline show up again in another story, do you think it would cause problems between him and Liberty?

RUGGED HEARTS

The Kinnison Legacy, Book I

by

AMANDA MCINTYRE

Chapter One

A blustery, forty-mile-an-hour north wind sliced across the pasture, pelting razor-sharp pellets of ice at Wyatt Kinnison's face. He narrowed his eyes to protect them from the bitter attack as he set to the task of freeing the squirming calf from the barbed wire wrapped around its leg. Controlling his anger, he whistled softly between his teeth, a habit he'd picked up from his stepdad. He inspected the wriggling creature, relieved to see only a portion of hair had rubbed off its hide. The cantankerous runt reminded him of his younger brother. Even now that he was older, it seemed he was forever pulling Dalton's butt out of a wringer. "This is the third time this week I've saved your sorry ass," he cautioned the calf. "You may not be so lucky next time."

Circumstances had caused Wyatt to become an adult long before he should have, and it had left him tainted. He had little patience with children or ornery calves, but like his brother, he'd give his life for them.

"Dammit, do me a favor. Hold still." He clenched his jaw from both frustration and cold. The exposed flesh on the side of his neck was numb where the frigid wind and snow had blown down his collar. The calf twisted in his grasp, bawling woefully with the sudden movement. He could have just snipped the fence, but with the darkening sky and the wind blurring his vision, he didn't want to risk greater injury to the animal. This close to the mountains, one could never be sure what predators roamed the woods, their senses alert to the scent of fresh blood. "There, you little troublemaker." He swatted the calf's butt and watched as he stumbled to stand on his wobbly legs. A call from the herd had the runt kicking up his heels, his tail flicking high, as he trotted with not a care in the world toward the sound of his mama's voice.

"You're welcome," Wyatt called out. "Stay close to your mom. Maybe it'll keep you out of trouble." He let out a derisive snort, as if he had the slightest idea what it was like to be close to his mother. He had only been eleven and his brother Dalton, nine, when their mother had left them high and dry. Time had made him realize that maybe, in the end, she'd done them all a favor. But it didn't make the sting of finding her good-bye note on Christmas morning any easier. The holiday had never meant much to him after that.

Yeah, helluva Christmas present.

Wyatt pushed aside the painful thought and tugged the brim of his Stetson to block the wind. Flipping up the collar of his coat, he reached for the skewed post, set it upright, and then used the side of a short-handled ax to drive the pole into the sodden ground. He tamped the loose soil around the base with the heel of his boot and made a mental note to check the rest of the line come morning. Lifting his gaze, he scanned the opposite side of the pasture where the low pine-covered hills gave rise to the Crazies mountain range. The land, most of it owned by Last Hope Ranch, was one of the few remaining cattle ranches in the area. Near the Continental Divide, the acreage stretched from the mountain base to the closest town, End of the Line, Montana—population two hundred thirty-three at last count. Known in its day as a stop for traders and ranchers, the birth of the railway and the discovery of gold turned it into a virtual ghost town until some enterprising folks, including Jed, Wyatt's stepdad, found value in its rich western heritage and began the task of renovating its historical integrity. Growth hadn't always been swift, but for the folks in End of the Line, slow and steady was a lifestyle.

There were times, however, that Wyatt questioned Jed's decision to leave him as head of the ranch, but little else meant as much. He blew out a breath, glanced up at the gray-white, snow-filled sky, and thought of the man who'd taught him all he knew, who'd given him a new life. He slid the ax inside its worn leather harness and pulled himself up into the saddle. Holding on to his hat, he ducked his head from the charge of driving wind and snow. He'd feel a lot better when this deal to sell off the heifers was firmly in place. With another quick glance at the herd huddled under a giant oak, he turned away from the wind. He drew his glove over his face, wiped the snow from his eyelashes, and nudged the horse toward home. She fell into a steady trot, as eager as Wyatt to go where it was warm. The memory of the day Jed had surprised him with the horse flashed into his mind.

"It's time, son. You've earned this." Jed held out the reins, and Wyatt, not quite thirteen, took them with trembling hands. She was a beautiful Bay, almost sixteen hands high, with large, expressive, brown eyes that watched him closely as he drew near. He laid his cheek against her neck, and she nuzzled the back of his head. He named her Pretty Lady, after a comment Jed had made about her graceful looks. She was the first female he'd ever truly loved.

Years later, he realized Jed must have known how the mare's even temper and strength would be a lesson to a boy nursing the scars of his mother's abandonment. He leaned forward and brushed the snow from her soft brown coat. There were times he could swear she could read his mind as well as he could hers. "Come on, Lady, I hear a bucket of oats calling your name." Attentive to what he said, the horse pricked her ears and quickened her pace. The weather caused his thoughts to turn briefly to his younger brother Dalton, and

Rein, Jed's nephew. The three were a family, raised from their teen years to manhood by Jed, a self-made man with no children of his own and possessing a heart as big as a Montana Sky. He'd adopted Wyatt and Dalton shortly after marrying their mom, and after she left, it wasn't more than a year later when Rein, a quiet, studious young man, had come to live with his uncle after his parents had been killed in a car accident.

The two would-be brothers had just left on their annual trip to Sioux City, where they brokered the sales of some of their cattle to a client that had traded with Jed for years. The pilot they'd hired to travel to the meeting was a former Iraqi soldier and good friend who now ran a small charter company out of Billings. Wyatt was glad to have heard from Rein, even though the news wasn't what he'd expected.

"There's been a delay," Rein said. "Some of the numbers on the contract aren't what we originally discussed. I want to talk to this new attorney and see what's going on. The problem is it seems this guy took off on an impromptu ski trip and won't be back until the day after tomorrow."

"So much for flying down early to cinch this up before the holiday. Why not just talk to the guy by phone or use that Skype thing you talk so much about?" Wyatt wasn't particularly concerned about spending Christmas by himself. Over the years, he'd spent many a holiday alone, while the other two, off at college, took full advantage of things like spring break and ski trips.

"Not this time, bro. I'm concerned about the figures on this agreement. They aren't what I remember them to be. I want to talk to the guy face-to-face. We may be going back to the drawing board. I think he's trying to finagle things a bit to pad his pockets, and I don't think ol' Russ is aware of it just yet. The poor guy is in his eighties and still trading like he did when Jed worked with him. I want a good deal, but I want it to be fair for all of us. I plan to speak to him, though, before his legal counsel gets back to town."

It was useless to argue. Rein was the one with the business

head and dual degrees in agricultural business and architectural design under his shiny silver belt buckle. He'd returned home with the intention of seeing to fruition his uncle's vision for the ranch, to make it a haven for the lost and weary and a place to find purpose and strength through nature and hard work. It was an idea born of a man who'd reared three dysfunctional teens, not of his blood, and turned them into capable young men whom he was proud to call his sons.

"Just keep me posted. How's Dalton taking the delay?"

Rein snorted. "About like you'd think. He's afraid he's going to miss the annual holiday pool tourney at the pub."

Wyatt shook his head, thinking of his younger brother. Twice his size, Dalton looked like some mountain man with an unruly beard and black, curly hair. He had barely squeaked through college and afterward took off to travel and find himself. He'd never been as devoted to the ranch as the other two, but somehow a couple of years later he found himself back home, still fighting his demons and still unsure of what to do with his life. Nonetheless, Wyatt's maturity gave him the ability to see and appreciate qualities in his younger brother; he viewed him akin to a slightly misguided knight, trying to right the injustices of the world. Dalton, like Rein, believed in the vision that Jed had for Last Hope Ranch, but Wyatt was less excited about changing the way things were. He enjoyed the solitude and let the other two handle the networking necessities.

"Let me know what's going on, Rein, and keep an eye on the weather."

"Right. Talk to you soon."

က

Wyatt shifted in the saddle, happy when he finally saw the faint lights of home through the swirling snow. "Almost there, girl." He looked at the ranch, spread out like a sparkling jewel in the valley. Jed would talk with pride about designing and building the home and how for every tree used in construction, he'd plant two more on the property. Its true purpose was his intention of raising a large family and the hope of many grandkids. Instead, Jed wound up divorced with three misfit boys to raise. He had been not only a brilliant rancher but also an eternal optimist. When he saw the need for the children of End of the Line to have visit each year from Kris Kringle, he'd filled that need and so too, his own need for a bigger family. He referred to the children over the years as "his kids." There'd been a time or two as Jed grew older that he voiced regret that Wyatt wasn't able to give him his own grandkids to spoil, but settling down as a family man had never been one of Wyatt's goals.

"You've got to let go of the past," his stepdad had told him after the breakup of his first real relationship. It had lasted only three weeks. "You've got to learn to trust others, Wyatt. Trust your heart."

He'd listened to Jed on many things, never doubting his wisdom, but in this, Wyatt ignored him. He knew where his loyalties were. Maybe it was true what he said about letting go of the past and all of its baggage, but it was easier to put his heart into something solid and reliable, like running the ranch. Uncomfortable with such thoughts, he switched his focus to getting home and the delicious the crock-pot stew awaiting him. With thoughts of a toasty fire, some mindless television, and a hearty supper, he nudged Lady's sides and broke into a gallop toward the barn.

With his horse brushed and happily fed, Wyatt finished his evening chores before securing the barn and heading out into the chilly night. He stuffed his hands in his pockets, listening to the sound of his boots crunching along the frosty ground. The wind rushing through the pines whistled softly. An odd pang of loneliness shot through his heart, and he brushed it quickly away as he trudged up the front steps to the cabin. The heavy thud of his boots on the wraparound wood porch pricked at his mind. The sound alone jarred a strange comfort inside of him, knowing he was home for the night. He walked around the corner of the house, where they kept wood stacked, and loaded a few logs into his arms. A sudden movement caught his eye. Tightening his grasp on the wood, he watched a great white owl sweep out of the sky, snatch something from the snowy ground, and disappear into the screen of trees. A low, ominous hoot poked at Wyatt's brain, and a shiver skated across his shoulders. The American Indian tribes living in the area believe the sight of an owl to be a sign of an impending storm. Wyatt chuckled and brushed off the strange feeling. Weather radar online dispelled many of the old superstitions, but it wouldn't hurt to check the forecast just in case.

೮౩

"That ought to last us a while." Pleased with the roaring fire, Wyatt pushed to his knees for a moment and drew Sadie, the family's golden retriever, to his side. "It doesn't get much better than this, Sadie girl." He grabbed the bowl of stew he'd prepared and took a large bite of the bread Rein had brought home from the bakery. He settled back on the couch, relishing the soft, aged leather, and lifted his stocking feet onto the coffee table, one of many woodworking projects Rein had built.

Sadie curled up dutifully beneath his legs, happy to have her master home after a long day. She was well over eight years old now, best they knew. Jed had found her on the side of the mountain road one autumn evening, and despite attempts to find her owner, nobody ever showed to claim her. It was a joyous fact that the three boys never took for granted. They cared for her, loving her like a member of the family and though she moved a little slower these days, she could still protect her family if necessary.

Wyatt picked up his bowl and breathed in the savory spices mingled with the roasted meat, potatoes, and carrots. He blew across the bowl, stirring slowly before lifting a generous portion to his mouth. He leaned forward, his attention diverted to the screen showing the bull-riding championships. Sadie's head popped up in alarm and bumped the back of Wyatt's outstretched legs. The spoon flipped from his grasp, bounced off his chest, and landed on his lap, leaving a beefy brown trail in its wake. "What the Sam Hill...?"

He glared at the frantic dog pacing back and forth across the wood floor. She began to bark, first at him, then at the direction of the front door. He brushed helplessly at his shirt, annoyed at both the stain and his wacky dog. Assuming it was the weather adversely affecting her behavior, he shook his head and watched with curious amusement as she attempted to get traction on the polished wood. "Okay, girl, fun's over. Time to settle down. Come on, Sadie. You just heard an owl. There's nothing out there."

She paused a moment glancing at him as if to ask, "are you sure" when an urgent knock sounded, renewing the dog's duty to protect. She stood with her nose against the heavy barrier separating them from the intruder outside, offering a clear warning to whoever waited on the other side.

Wyatt swept a glance over the cabinet where they kept their hunting rifles locked up. He quickly shoved aside the concern and headed across the room. "Settle down, Sadie. I'll take care of this." He flipped on the porch light and grabbed the anxious dog by her collar as he opened the door. As he straightened, his gaze followed a pair of shapely legs and a heart-shaped butt encased in denim jeans with rhinestones on the pockets. She couldn't have been from the area because the sugar-pink puff jacket she wore barely covered her waist. A local would know it wasn't adequate for Montana winters.

The woman turned abruptly, and his gaze snapped up and held hers as he quickly tried to set aside his lusty thoughts. He held tight to the squirming dog with one hand and pushed open the glass storm door against the pounding wind with the other. Her eyes widened as she looked him over head to toe, and he saw her hesitation as she glanced down at Sadie's determined wiggling.

"She's more bark than bite." He tried to reassure her, but the wariness lingered. She had her hands stuffed in the pockets, and he zeroed in to the tense way she licked her lower lip, her breath forming frosty puffs in the icy air. Despite finding this lovely pink package on his front porch on a cold winter's night, Wyatt, too, was a bit wary. Very few folks ever paid a visit to the ranch, and even fewer women. However, if she was looking for someone, likely it was his younger brother. Of the three of them, it was Dalton who had a reputation with the ladies, and on occasion, their boyfriends didn't appreciate it. Going on that assumption, he looked over her shoulder at her vehicle. It was clearly not for serious mountain driving in adverse weather, unless it happened to have a team of horses strapped to it. "Sorry, young lady. Dalton's not home."

She blinked and gave him an odd look.

"Excuse me?" She questioned his frank and admittedly unsocial behavior through chattering teeth. "I don't know any Dalton, but I'd like to meet him if he happens to have a map."

The woman obviously had no fear of being out alone in this weather, nor did it seem she was afraid to knock on any door of any strange house out in the middle of nowhere.

"Listen, I'm sorry to be a bother, but I want to make sure I'm on the right road. It seems maybe I might have missed my turnoff. Are you familiar with the town of End of the Line?" she asked, stomping the snow from her faux-fur fashion boots.

The winding mountain road was dotted with an array of old mining towns with fewer than fifty or so residents and End of the Line happened to be one of the largest. "Sure, I know where it is." Her cheeks and the tip of her nose were pink from the cold. She smiled and sniffled, and it pulled Wyatt from his reverie. "Pardon my manners. Why don't you come inside and get out of the cold." To her credit, he saw the hesitation in her eyes before she stepped around him and into the foyer. The scent of peppermint and winter air tickled his nose, and he noted sprigs of blond hair sticking out from beneath the furry rim of her hood. Sadie leaped up and placed her paws on the woman's chest.

"I'm sorry. She's really quite friendly."

The woman pushed her face to Sadie's and ruffled her fur. "She's a sweetheart, she is," the woman cooed, apparently forgetting he was standing there.

Wyatt cleared his throat and reached out to move Sadie down, though it seemed the two females had become fast friends.

"I went down to Big Timber for the day," the woman began. "Then this snow started just out of the blue." She waved her hands as she spoke.

No gloves, just as he'd thought.

"Between the dark and the snow, I'm not sure if I'd already passed by my turn to town. Thankfully, I saw your lights from the road and took a chance someone might be home."

"Isn't it a bit risky for someone your age to be out alone on night like this?" He frowned as he shut the door. He leaned back against it and folded his arms over his chest in the same fatherly manner he'd seen Jed display a million times.

Her gaze shot to his, and she pushed off her hood, raking her fingers through her hair, sending spiky, short-clipped platinum blond tresses in all directions. He wasn't much for short hair on women and frankly preferred dark to light hair. But on her, it seemed to fit with her slight build and mesmerizing blue eyes, which, he noted, appeared a whole lot less innocent at the moment.

She chuckled. "So what are you? Just some cowboy serial killer just chillin' here by the fire and waiting for your next victim?"

Put in those terms, it seemed like a pretty stupid concept.

She fished in her jacket pocket, and as she retrieved a tissue, a little blue mitten fell out. "Hopefully that wasn't the line you used to pick up your wife."

Wait a minute, do I look like a married man?

She bent over and so did he to retrieve the mitten.

"Did I say I was married?"

Maybe she was the one who was married. Then again, she looked very young. He scooped up the mitten and handed it to her.

"Uh, no, I just assumed." She shrugged, not meeting his eyes.

"Assumed?"

She licked her lips. "Based on your age and all."

My age?

"Hey, but at least you're the gentlemanly serial-killer type."

Wyatt released a sigh. This conversation was spinning wildly out of control. "Of course I'm not a serial killer."

"That's a relief," she muttered.

"Look, I was trying to make a point." He wanted to explain that she was mistaken about the wife thing, but he didn't have a clue why it should matter one way or another.

"Yeah, I appreciate your concern." She stuffed the mitten in her coat pocket and swiped the Kleenex under her pert nose. "But news flash, I'm not as young as I look and I guess one day I'll be grateful for those genetics. Right now it's frustrating, particularly at bars and with people like you."

"Like me?" This woman was spry, but her attitude more than made up for her size. "What do you mean? I'm trying to be the nice guy here."

"Listen, mister. I teach a second-grade class and if you don't think you have to be tough, I invite you to try one day with them." She looked him over. "They'd chew you up. No offense."

"None taken." He frowned, finding her spunk sexier than he should.

"All I need is for you to tell me the name of the road that I need to turn on to get back to town and then you can return to planning who your next victim will be." She smiled and damn if there wasn't a twinkle in her eye.

Mouthy as all hell. He pinned her with a puzzled look.

"Listen, lady, for the record, not everyone up in these mountains is as hospitable as me. Besides, don't you carry a map in your car?"

Her gaze narrowed. She brushed an errant strand of blond hair from her eye. "If you're the best in hospitable these mountains have to offer, no wonder everyone calls it the land that time forgot. And no, Mr. Triple-A police, I don't happen to have a map in my car. It didn't come in the welcome wagon basket."

Wyatt eyed her, not knowing whether to help her or toss her cute behind out in the snow. He figured, though, he'd brought on some of her saucy attitude. "The Git and Go in town keeps them right by the counter," he tossed out, the sparring between them eliciting a tingling of arousal. By God, that hadn't happened since his old girlfriend, Jessie, a mistake he had no intention of making again. Wyatt carefully reeled in his wayward emotions, holding his gaze steady on hers in a display of wills.

She chewed the corner of her lip and then raised an eyebrow. "Good to know. Okay then, this conversation has been riveting, if not educational, but I'll not take up any more of your time. I think I may have tapped out your quota of hospitality for the season." She reached around him and grabbed the doorknob. He moved aside, flustered why he felt so agitated. Hadn't she heard a word he was trying to say? "Listen, obviously you're new around here."

She glanced up at him. Her arched brow spoke volumes.

"It's just that these storms can pop up rather unexpectedly through the mountains, kind of like a squall. Half the time radar doesn't even catch them until it's on top of us. When you've lived here long enough, you'll know better to be prepared before venturing out." It was clear from the way her blue eyes scalded him that she didn't appreciate his speech on safety. He glanced down at his feet and kicked himself for sounding like her father. It was a gut reaction. If something needed to be fixed, he approached it without hesitation and used his common sense. To those who didn't know him very well, he supposed that he could sound a bit overbearing, perhaps even bossy. From the look on her face, he'd nailed both pretty good. Her smile was tolerant at best.

"Do you know the name of the road or not? I'm tired, I'm lost, and frankly I don't need the fatherly lecture." She held tight to the doorknob, eyeing him a second more, then flipped up her hood and yanked on the door. "Never mind, I'll find it, thanks."

He swiped a hand over his mouth, sensing what he was about to do was not be a good idea. He put his hand over hers. Having sworn off dating for more time than he cared to admit, he was admittedly out of practice with how to handle a female—a tired and feisty one, at that.

Her back stiffened and those blue eyes snapped to his, flashing thunderbolts. He dropped his hand, trying to decide whether he needed to raise his fists or not. "Okay. There's no need to get all riled up. Simmer down. I'm just trying to give you a few tips in survival up here in these mountains. Give me a second. I think I may have an extra map. It will be easier to show you where the turnoff is."

"Simmer down? Right, cowboy." Her mocking whisper was as good as a slap to the back of his head.

Maybe he had it coming.

"Nice place you have here," she called from the entrance to the great room. The vaulted ceiling carried her voice through the rafters.

He glanced up and saw her taking in the rustic interior. "My father...um, stepdad, built it."

"Impressive." She careened her head back to look overhead. "I think my apartment alone could fit in this room maybe—five times over."

Wyatt retrieved an old map and walked toward her, letting his gaze travel up the tilt of her neck as she gazed up at the ceiling. Her chin dropped suddenly and her eyes met his. Zing! Wyatt nearly stumbled over his feet at the impact. He covered his faux pas by blaming poor Sadie and clearing his throat, handed the girl the map. Nope, cowboy, you do not want to go there. However, his treacherous body, too long without a woman next to it, had entirely different ideas. Wyatt steered his mind from heading down that dangerous path. "You want to take the lane out here back to the main road."

She tossed him a dubious look. "Amazingly, I figured as much." She opened the map, folded it, and moved to his side. "Now what?"

Damn, if she hadn't taken the words right out of his mouth. He glanced down and decided the sooner he got her on her way, the better for both of them. "You turn right at the top of the hill, then go north on eighty-nine. In about five miles you should see a sign on the right, for the scenic overlook."

She nodded. "Okay, yep, I remember it. I just couldn't recall the name."

"It's county road forty-five and it ought to be clear. Dusty's bar is at that end of town. He likes to keep the secondary road open for his customers. Usually does it himself."

"You think he's still open?" she asked, busily refolding the map.

He bit his tongue, wanting to advise her about going alone into the old pub. He knew firsthand the sort of unsavory characters who sometimes came in from other towns. There were a lot of guys who frequented the place. Most looking for a good time. He should know, it was how he met Jessie, the woman he thought he'd spend the rest of his life with. He'd given his heart to her completely, only to discover a couple of months later that not only did guys go to Dusty's to find a little fun, so did Jessie. Suffice it to say he hadn't been back to Dusty's in over a year, and the whole affair had left him with a bitter taste in his mouth about dating. He swept his gaze over the woman as she prepared to leave and wondered how many hearts she'd left in her wake. "I've never known Dusty to close early for any reason, especially on a night like this. He believes travelers out there might need a hot meal or a place to stay."

"He seems like a nice man." She didn't say whether or not she had plans to stop there. "Okay, great, thanks again. Sorry to have bothered you." She presented him with the map.

"Keep it. You never know when you might need it again." When she turned her back, he made a face at how his comment probably sounded and hoped she hadn't caught it.

"By the way...." She turned on her heel and with a decisive poke with the map nailed him in the chest. "You've been so generous with your advice let me give you some." She pressed her face close enough that it sent his brain scrambling. "Try a little lemon juice on those beef stains." She trailed the map down his shirt and tossed him a wink before sprinting out the door to her car.

The wind nearly tore the storm door from his hand as he watched her climb into her car. "Drive safely." Stunned by her blatant comment, his response, too late, was swallowed by the wind. He stared after her and realized she hadn't asked his name, nor offered hers. He wasn't terribly surprised in retrospect, given that he'd treated her like she was twelve. Something about her jangled his nerves. Maybe it was her attitude that reminded him of Jessie and his defenses just shot up. He followed the headlights as they bounced up the lane and disappeared from sight and then closed the door. "Like I'll ever have to worry about running into her again, right girl?" He ruffled the dog's fur. "Do I look like a serial killer to you?"

A small laugh escaped his lips. He sauntered back to the coffee table, thinking about the strange encounter and the fact that he'd probably need to reheat his stew. To his surprise, he found the dish empty—clean as a whistle. Sadie wagged her tail as though to say thanks for the treat, then realizing his displeasure, ducked her head and slunk back to her bed, where she curled up and looked up at him with a woeful expression. Her soft brown gaze shot to his, silently pleading for absolution. Isn't that just like a female? With the face of an angel they sucker you in and the next thing you know you're in a world of hurt. Thinking back to his recent encounter with that pair of eyes the color of a summer sky, staring up at him for help, Wyatt released an uneasy sigh. Sure as the north wind blowing fierce outside, he felt the swirl of the impending storm stirring inside of him.

ঙ

Aimee gripped the steering wheel and tried to convince herself her body's uncontrolled trembling had more to do with the cold than her unplanned meeting of the dark-eyed cowboy. She fumbled with the heat, one eye on the view in front of her, and tried to see where the snow had drifted across the road. Abandoning her efforts to stay warm, she leaned forward to stay focused, watching the snow-matted signs so she wouldn't miss her turn, but her mind slipped back to the stranger's dark hair and how it curled slightly over his flannel shirt collar. Those gravy stains on his white T-shirt were hard to miss, and she realized she'd interrupted his dinner. Probably just in from his chores, he had that comfortable in-for-the-evening look about him in his worn jeans and unbuttoned shirt that flashed ideas of snuggling on a couch on such a cold night. She hadn't seen any photos indicating a wife or kids as she waited for him to retrieve the map, but given his bristly attitude, she wondered if he'd recently come out of a difficult relationship. He seemed to be a man of integrity, appeared successful, and Lord in heaven, from a pure physical standpoint, he was her idea of a cowboy, from his honed muscles and the perfect fit of his worn jeans to the glint in his espresso-colored eyes. And he was doing well. Any doubt of that was cinched when she walked into the spacious great room. With a cathedral ceiling, it was a gorgeous blend of a rustic lodge and modern comfort. Honey-colored pine rafters formed the open framework, running the entire length of the ceiling. Two leather couches faced one another in front of a massive, handcrafted stone fireplace and a set of wingbacks upholstered in a rich black-and-red plaid rounded out the warm and inviting seating arrangement. Massive woven area rugs, in reds, golds, browns, most probably handcrafted by local American Indian artisans, accentuated the gleam of the warm, polished dark wood floors. It was as grand as anything Aimee had ever seen. Her head was on a swivel as she took in the floor-to-ceiling bookshelves and the wall of windows across the back of the room. A large-screen television hung over the grand fireplace and what looked like an open office area overlooked the back of the house. She felt as though she'd walked into a layout of American Cowboy magazine. How in the world had she missed seeing such a tall, cool drink of fine in town?

The sight of a large buck standing at the edge of the road snapped her back to the present. No match for him in her Subaru, she slowed and waited, her eyes darting back and forth to the rearview mirror, hoping no one would come around the bend and rear-end her. The animal's ebony eyes sparkled in the glare of her headlights and she swore he was looking right through the front window, defiantly challenging which of them would move first. He turned his head majestically over his shoulder and a female deer with two fawn appeared, inching cautiously to his side and then past him. His head came up and his gaze met Aimee's as his family crossed the road, blending into the darkness on the other side. She stared in rapt fascination at the protective way he watched them. Then, when he was certain of their safety, he followed, ignoring Aimee's presence entirely. Her heart beat in wild exhilaration at the sight. Aside from her recent encounter, it was the first exciting thing that had happened to her since moving to this remote area. She had to admit, there was a stirring in her blood as she noted the remarkable likeness of the stag's intense gaze to the cowboy she'd just met. Aimee eased the car forward and realized suddenly she'd been so flustered by the circumstances that she'd forgotten to ask his name. Perhaps more disappointing, however, was he hadn't bothered to ask hers. Still, the overprotection of a complete stranger was endearing, in an old-fashioned way. Surely, someone in town could tell her about him.

She drove carefully down the narrow road, flanked either side with pine trees, grateful that someone with a large truck had driven through the pass recently, leaving a clear path for her to follow. "Finally," she said with a sigh when she saw the outline of Fred's Garage at the edge of town. Not much farther, should be this place called Dusty's. She'd known about it, but had wondered if, as the new second-grade teacher, it would be wise to frequent such a place. However, in End of the Line, it seemed to be the only place to socialize besides Betty's Café. She hoped it wouldn't be too busy on a night like this. A quiet drink sounded good. She slowed and searched the array of pickup trucks parked in the gravel lot.

The pink neon light flashing Dusty's was an enticing welcome to her frazzled nerves. She passed the first drive, battling the wisdom of turning in, and saw her last chance looming beyond a short snowdrift, a few feet ahead. With a sigh, she yanked on the wheel and pulled her car into a spot between two massive pickup trucks. She sat for a moment, still debating the social consequences, but her need for a peaceful drink outweighed the potential for scandal. She locked the door, hooked her purse over her shoulder, and headed for the front door, almost dissuaded by the catcalls of two older men who were leaving. She ignored them, pulled open the door, and hoped at least one of them was sober enough to drive. The music of the jukebox blared in the near-empty room and she felt the stiffness in her shoulders relax. Raucous male laughter filtered in from the back room, where she surmised a pool table must be. Cautiously, she unzipped her jacket and looked for a quiet spot where she could be alone. She spotted a seat at the end of the bar. A couple sat in one of the corner booths, so wrapped up in each other that Aimee decided the place could be on fire and they wouldn't notice. Yet other than the couple, those involved in a pool game, and the bartender, the bar was virtually empty.

"Welcome to Dusty's." The man behind the polished

counter greeted her with a friendly smile and went on with stacking clean glasses on the shelves. "I'm Dusty. What can I get you?"

Aimee slipped off her coat and placed it on the back of the stool. She looked up and caught the man studying her.

"Stinger, on the rocks," she answered. "You know how to make one?"

His brows rose and he nodded. "Sure thing. Comin' right up." He began to put the drink together.

"Is there a problem?" she asked, sliding into her seat, beginning to regret her impulsive decision.

He shrugged. "Not at all. Forgive me. I make it a point of knowing my customers. This is your first time here, am I right?"

She nodded.

"You're that second-grade teacher up to school? Saw your picture in the paper after you came to town." He tossed her a smile.

Aimee propped her forearms on the rolled leather rest of the bar and gave the man a pointed look. "That's me, and at the risk of starting all kinds of rumors, my nerves are a bit frazzled by what I've just driven through. I'm sort of celebrating getting back here, unscathed, before I head on home. You okay with that?" She pushed a hand through her hair. "Sorry, I don't mean to sound like a—" She stopped herself. It was enough she was here; she probably shouldn't add cussing to the rumor mill.

"Sounds like the lady needs a drink, Dusty." She looked to her left and found a handsome face with an equally charming smile. His eyes were a startling blue and he wore his thick, wavy hair combed back over his ears. Broad shoulders filled out his too-small black T-shirt with a faded Metallica logo on the front. He perched his boot on the foot rail and leaned on his elbow, his gaze focused on her. He looked perfectly at home.

The barkeep scooted her drink across on a napkin. "Five-fifty," he stated, picking up his towel. Aimee fished through her purse in search of her pocketbook.

"Let me get this, darlin'." Mr. Metallica slapped a ten on the bar and gave her a cocky grin.

The predatory glint in his eye made it obvious where he hoped his gesture would go.

"That isn't necessary." She started to pull her money out.

He smacked a hand to his heart. "I realize, sweetheart, but there are so few times when I've had the good fortune to meet an angel in the flesh."

Dusty chuckled and Aimee offered the stranger a congenial smile. Clearly, he was well practiced in the art of pick-up lines.

"Steve? You gonna play or what?" One of the guys came in from the back room, a pool cue resting on his shoulder. He passed Aimee a glance.

"Don't suppose you play pool, do you, angel?" Mr. Metallica asked, his eyes looked her over as his lip curved in a come-hither smile.

Aimee shook her head and swirled the ice cubes in her drink. She wished he'd take his friend's invitation to return to the game.

He leaned closer, his grin blossoming into a full-blown, sexy smile. Maybe it was the drink, the storm, or the aftereffects of the handsome cowboy lingering still in her mind, but damn, to a woman wanting to be held for a while, this guy was seriously tempting.

"Well, if my luck holds out, maybe you'll be here when I get through?"

She offered him a smile. "I don't think so." He slid his fingers over hers, letting them linger on her skin. Charming was one thing, pushy another.

"You're sure?" He lowered his voice.

"Steve, come on man! We've got money riding on this one."

"Quite." She slid her hand from his.

He stood, towering over her, giving her one last look at his powerfully sexy physique. "Maybe another time. My friends and I come up here a lot. The food...is excellent." He tossed the bartender a look.

"You best get on in there, Steve." Dusty nodded toward the friend who waited impatiently at the back-room door. "They'll be starting without you."

He swaggered toward the door, and then glanced over his shoulder with a parting, impish grin.

"Good Lord," she muttered and finished her drink.

"Mind if I offer a piece of friendly advice?" Dusty spoke, his focus intent on the pilsner he polished.

Aimee hopped off the stool and slid into her jacket. "You mean about Steve? Yeah, I know a player when I see one, no worries." She tugged her purse over her shoulder. "But thank you for keeping an eye on a girl."

A slow smile crept over the bartender's face. "He and his buddies live a few miles down the road. They come in a couple of times a week to play pool. You okay to drive home?"

"Yeah, I'm good. Thanks, Dusty."

"Come on back anytime."

Aimee smiled. Unless she was with someone, the chances were slim. She stopped at the end of the bar and turned to him. "Say, listen. Maybe you can help me out with something. You said you know a lot of folks around here?"

He shrugged. "Seems eventually, they all come through here. I've got the only jukebox and bar for miles around."

She chewed her lip and wondered whether it was wise to inquire openly about the stranger on the ranch. What could it hurt? The worst thing she'd possibly find out was that he was married, recently divorced, or engaged in some bitter custody battle over his kids. She took a breath and charged ahead. "I was wondering about something...someone, actually."

"I'll do my best."

"Well, I stopped to get directions at this place up the road. Looks like a giant ski lodge down in the valley...south a little ways, just off eighty-nine."

He nodded. "Yeah, I'm guessing you mean Last Hope Ranch. Fine looking place. Jed Kinnison, God rest his soul, and those three boys created quite a cattle business down there. Hard workers, all of them."

Aimee swallowed. "There's more than one?" She tried not to sound giddy. "I only met one of them. He's got dark hair, intense, kind of bossy." She gave him a half smile. "Very bossy."

"Yeah, that'd be the oldest of Jed's boys—Wyatt. I heard Dalton and Rein had left on their annual sales trip."

"Sales?" she asked, her mind simmering still on the old-fashioned name of Wyatt.

"Yep, Last Hope is one of the last working cattle ranches in these parts. Has been for as long as I've been around. Every winter they sell off some of the herd to feedlots down in Iowa and Missouri."

"But Wyatt isn't involved in...the sales?" Bartenders were a lot like beauticians, Aimee discovered. Get them started and they could dish on about anybody.

He chuckled. "Not Wyatt. No, he prefers to stay home, keep an eye on things at the ranch. Kind of a loner but a nice enough guy. Quiet. Now you take his younger brother, Dalton. There's a social guy. You'd like him. Flirts like hell, loves to dance and kid around, but he has a good heart. The boy would give you the shirt off his back. They all would. Jed raised some real fine men."

"Sounds like you have a lot of respect for them." Aimee adjusted her purse and started to leave, her attention drawn momentarily to the loud ruckus going on in the back room.

Dusty glanced toward the sound, sighed, and waited for the noise to settle before he spoke. "Jed, rest his soul, did lot for this community. Rein is the third of Jed's brood. His nephew that came to live with him when his folks were killed. Now there's a guy with a head for business. He helped me get this place back on track after I hit a rough patch. Jed raised the three as brothers, left himself quite a legacy in these parts."

Aimee smiled, even more curious why it was she'd never heard any of them mentioned by her peers at school. Still, she supposed teachers and ranchers didn't necessarily run in the same circles, unless of course they taught their children. Which left a question burning in the mind of any red-blooded, single woman. Were any of them married? That was a question for her friend, Sally. "Thanks, Dusty."

She waved a quick good-bye and hurried to her car. The snow had slowed to intermittent flakes by the time she climbed in and turned on the ignition to warm it up. She glanced at her watch and realized she had just enough time to get home and register for the online poetry class she promised Sally she'd take. Aside from her duties as End of the Line's elementary music teacher, Sally moonlighted as an online instructor through Billings Community College. She spotted the map on the seat, picked it up, and thought of Wyatt's sincere concern for her safety. True he hadn't smiled much...at all, in fact, but his gaze was kind, if not tinged with a puzzling look that made her want to know more about what he'd been thinking. Still, in the entire time she was alone with him, she never felt threatened, as she had around Mr. Metallica in a public bar.

Aimee tucked the map into the console between the seats and eased her car out onto the main road. For as early as it was in the evening, she could've shot cannon down the street. Like a scene from *It's A Wonderful Life*, the store fronts were dark, in contrast to the festive holiday wreaths waving in the wintery challenge of the wind. Small white lights dotted the branches of the dwarf trees along the businesses, twinkling with each northerly breeze. A twinge of melancholy hit her. She missed not being at home with her parents, especially this time of year. She wondered at the wisdom in accepting a job in a place so remote that it was truly worthy of its name—End of the Line.

She glanced down at the map and remembered the

encounter earlier with Wyatt Kinnison. An interesting man and a challenge if ever there was one, if what she'd heard about him was true at all. Then again, she'd never backed away from obstacles before. Maybe there was more to why she was there than she'd considered. After all, it was the season of miracles.

~ABOUT THE AUTHOR~

Photography by Kimberly Rocha

Growing up the daughter of a father who was a distributor for a New York Magazine Publishing firm, Amanda usually had her nose stuck in the latest issue of Vampirella or a Hitchcock Mystery book. An artist first, her penchant for creating started at an early age with crayons and colored pencils and much of what she learned makes her a 'visual' writer. A renaissance woman, she has worked in the corporate world, written a weekly newspaper column supporting Fine Arts in our schools, loves to travel, do research and perhaps her greatest achievement—raised four kids.

Amanda has been referred to as a "true artist in the writing realm' and her zest for life inspires her "character-driven" stories. Her passion is to take ordinary people and place them in extraordinary situations, delving into the realm of potential and possibility as she watches them become the heroes and heroines of their own stories. She counts herself fortunate to be able to do what she loves, aspires to stay fresh and unique to her voice and listen to her readers. A member of RWA, and a multi-genre hybrid author, her work is published internationally, in audio, in e-book and in print. She currently writes sizzling contemporary and erotic historical romance.

Learn more about Amanda and join her social networks, newsletter, and street team at:
http://www.amandamcintyresbooks.com

Wild and Unruly
Tales of the Sweet Magnolia, Book I

Single, misjudged, and socially sequestered, library curator Lillian White lives vicariously through her beloved books of the bawdy Old West, dreaming of the cowboy that will take her away from her lonely life until the day she discovers a mysterious, antique necklace with the power to tap into her deepest desires and possibly change her life forever.

Sheriff Jake Sloan is Deadwater Gulch's "good son." A man married to the law, his heart secretly yearns for the Magnolia's headmistress, a soiled dove forbidden to him and his perfect reputation, until he saves her life from a ruthless gunman and injured, winds up convalescing in her bed.

Can a librarian with secret fantasies, make it as a bordello madam? And can a sheriff with his career in the balance fall in love with her? Be careful what you wish for...you just might get it.

"A charming tale with intriguing twists and a hero who's as noble as he is sizzling hot—you'll fall in love!" ~**Eden Bradley, 2010 Holt Medallion author of Pleasures Edge**

Fallen Angel
Tales of the Sweet Magnolia, Book II

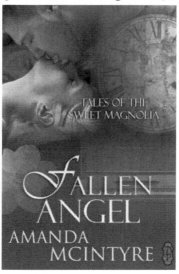

A hunger gnaws at Angel Marie Sutter to find the man behind the soulful music she heard played on the piano at the Sweet Magnolia. Following her heart, desire takes her on a fantastic journey. When she becomes a witness to murder, she finds herself under the forced protection of a scarred detective. Her gentle healing brings the past to his present in timeless passion, but will she be able to hold onto this precious gift, or will a killer take it all away?

Shado Jackson is a lone wolf undercover cop carrying guilt over the death of his brother. When a mysterious, beautiful woman becomes eyewitness to a murder, his job is to protect, not fall in love. But when his brother's killer again threatens to take what's precious from him, Shado must find him before time runs out.

"Very well written. I can't wait to read more in this series and more from Amanda McIntyre..."
~Romancing the Book Reviews

Made in the USA
San Bernardino, CA
16 September 2014